Chronicles of Air and Dreams

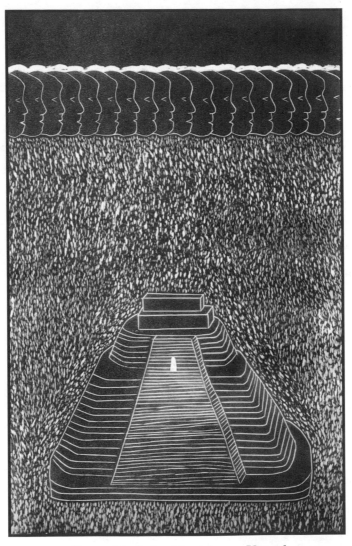

Pyramid of the Magician – Uxmal

Chronicles
of
Air and Dreams

A Novel of Mexico

Rosa Martha Villarreal

Archer Books

Published in the United States by:
Archer Books
P. O. Box 1254
Santa Maria, CA 93456

First edition

Publisher's Cataloging-in-Publication

Villarreal, Rosa Martha, 1955–
        Chronicles of air and dreams : a novel of Mexico /
    Rosa Martha Villarreal,
        p.   cm.
        ISBN 0-9662299-2-4
        1. Mexican Americans -- California -- San Jose
Fiction. 2. Mexico -- History -- Conquest, 1519-1540
Fiction.
        3. Indians of Mexico Fiction.   I. Title
        PS3572.I373C47 1999
        819' .54--dc21
                                                      99-3127
                                                          CIP

Printed in USA

Frontispiece: Linocut - Angela Tribulato

E-mail: books@archer-books.com
Web site: http://www.archer-books.com

In memory of my father,
Jaime Villarreal,
Coahuila storyteller

Acknowledgements

Special thanks to my husband, Dan Mizerski

. . . we only rise from a dream.

—Nezahualcóyotl

Everything changes so that
everything remains the same.

—A Mexican Saying

1

Beginnings

As in the time of the Mexican Conquest, the Dreamers were reborn in a collective visionary dream of a land with three moons. They witnessed enigmatic ceremonies inside a nebula of many colors; dreamed of flying over mountains of vertiginous heights and of navigating through oceans and rivers with their bodies.

In the villages of Mexico and in the shanty towns that flourished on the peripheries of Mexico City—all heavy with memories and the blood of Indians—these keepers of the ancient ways, elders and sorcerers alike, counted the signs as they appeared. The one they most anxiously awaited was the return of a woman called Malintzín. This woman, having the power of many languages, would be able to interpret their visionary dreams and translate the lost prophetic secrets of the Indians. These secrets, now reduced to mere rumors, said that following the reappearance of Malintzín, a spirit called Martín Cortés would become a man again and die a sacrificial death that would heal the scars of the Conquest by appeasing the gods of old. Others said that the last Aztec king, Cuauhtémoc, who had been hiding in the mountains for centuries, would join Martín Cortés in restoring the Indians to their former glory.

"She must be among us," said the Indian elders, convinced she would rise out of their masses.

They would be wrong.

One fetid summer day, in the Maya village of Palenque in southern Mexico, an American anthropology professor brought a team from State University of Pennsylvania to interview the village elders as part of his research on Mayan culture and iconography. With him was his graduate assistant, a young Mexican-American woman, brought along to serve as his translator.

The slender figure at the professor's side immediately provoked stares from the elders and villagers who saw her. Even from a distance, the elders discerned how the assistant's beauty transcended mere appearance, seeming to convert her body's very movements, and even the shadow it projected, into an apparition of feline-like elegance. Her long, Asiatic hair and almond-shaped green eyes struck the villagers and elders with a feeling of vague recognition, as if recalling her visage from a time long past, or even from a dream.

The young woman seemed to sense that something about her appearance was causing the agitated stares. When the professor introduced her to the elders, she acknowledged them with a nod and averted her green eyes, lowering her head as if to obstruct their curious probing.

Once the introductions were finished, the professor began the interview. The elders had brought their own interpreter to translate from Mayan to Spanish for the young woman, so that she could then translate from Spanish to English for the professor. To their astonishment, however, the young woman began translating directly to their language.

"You have several tongues," said one of the elders to her in Mayan.

As if the statement had broken a spell, the young woman looked at the elders directly, her smile filled with humility. "Yes," she responded in kind. "I speak six languages. It is my gift."

The elders, unable to contain their euphoria, murmured excitably among themselves.

"What's going on?" the professor asked his interpreter.

"I don't know," she said. "I can't hear what they're saying."

The elders stopped and again directed their attention to the young stranger.

"Do you possess the language of the old Mexicans?" asked another of the elders, referring to the Aztecs.

"Yes," she said.

"What is your name?" he asked.

She said, "My name is María Elena Vázquez."

The elders, possessing the ability to pierce the many frequencies of time, recognized that the moment for time to repeat itself had arrived. After a quick exchange of glances and nods, the most senior of them said, "We shall remember you, María Elena Vázquez, royal daughter."

By nightfall, there was not a single household in the village that did not know of the multilingual interpreter. They called her by her old name, Malintzín.

When the villagers went to market that weekend, they spoke of the beautiful young woman who possessed many languages. Thus, the speculative rumors about the return of Malintzín began to spread from market-place to marketplace, and to the many villages and hamlets of the region. At the festivals of the saints, and celebrations of holy days, the air was filled with wonder and speculation.

"Malintzín has returned."

"She will soon learn the secret language of the dead."

"No, she will be given the language of the very old ones."

"Who will teach her the new language?"

"The spirit of Martín Cortés, who stole the language while in his mother's belly."

By the end of summer, the people were heard saying, "Martín Cortés must now be near."

2

The Two Martíns

The conqueror of Mexico, the Captain-general and first *Marqués del Valle de Oaxaca*, Hernán Cortés, had two sons whom he named Martín. The firstborn Martín was the son he fathered with his interpreter, Malintzín. Born with his mother's beauty and the green eyes of a mystic, he found favor in his father's eyes.

That Hernán Cortés valued all of his offspring can be attested to by the fact that he eventually went to Rome and successfully petitioned the Pope to have all of his many bastard children legitimized. The name Martín, however, he had privately reserved for his heir, the one he intended to produce later after he had acquired a proper Spanish noblewoman for a wife. However, during the conquest of Mexico, with the passion stirred by the adventure of it all, and perhaps bewitched by the beauty of his Indian mistress, he dreamt that *this* son was to be named Martín.

The first Martín was but a small boy when his father took him to Spain, never again to see his mother. In their homeland, he was raised as a Spaniard, not as a *mestizo*—a person of mixed blood. Hernán had Martín trained in the military arts, and the son proved himself an able and crafty soldier. He fought beside his father during an expedition in Algiers, and later rescued him from drowning. Martín distinguished himself on the battlefield in Germany and Argel, earning the title, *Don* Martín Cortés, Commendador of the Order of St. James. *Don* Martín, who by this time, had a Spanish wife and children, would have been content to have continued his life and career in Spain. But he was forced to return to Mexico and find disgrace at the hands of his younger brother, also named Martín.

The second son of Hernán Cortés named Martín was the legal heir and second Marqués del Valle de Oaxaca. He was born thirteen years after his mixed blood half-brother to his father's second wife, the Spanish noble-woman Juana de Zuñiga. (*Don* Hernán married this second wife after the mysterious death of his first, Catalina Xuárez. Rumors circulated in New Spain that Hernán Cortés had murdered his sterile first wife, but charges were never brought forth.). Thus, the younger Martín was conceived and born under inauspicious and, some said, maledictory circumstances.

Spoiled by his mother and indulged by his father, the younger Martín did not grow up to be a soldier like his older brother, but a parasitic curiosity, a dandy in the Spanish royal court. Perhaps his father saw the young Martín's inherent weakness of character because he put his older brother in charge of protecting the younger.

16

Hernán Cortés accomplished this dishonorable feat by denying the older Martín any inheritance independent of the younger son.

In 1563, *Don* Martín the Commendador was ordered to accompany his younger brother to Mexico. Once there and established as the Second *Marqués del Valle*, the younger Martín continued on his reckless path. He threw lavish parties and masques and, although already married, flirted shamelessly with the ladies of the new Mexican *Criollo* aristocracy. He became fast friends with two brothers, Gil and Alonso Gonzáles de Ávila. Sons of conquistadors, the young *Criollos* overestimated their own importance. Somewhere in the midst of their revelries, the Gonzáles de Ávila brothers, the young Martín Cortés, and as many as one hundred other *Criollos* devised a plot to murder the Spanish viceroy and his officials and proclaim Mexico an independent kingdom. The young Martín was to become their king.

The elder Martín, who was not included in his brother's inner circle, was completely unaware of the plot and utterly shocked when he found himself under arrest for treason. Spanish justice was swift: the Gonzáles de Ávila brothers were beheaded, the elder Martín tortured and exiled to Spain. Curiously, the younger Martín was merely confined for life to the royal court in Spain, where his insignificance reduced him to a footnote in history.

The elder Martín disappeared, lost in history, but not in the chronicles of air and dreams. The true story of *Don* Martín, the eldest son of Hernán Cortés, prevailed in the windstorms and caverns of sleep. Many have dreamed it: Martín was accused of witchcraft. An inquisition was conducted. Through torture, damning testimony was extracted from other Indians that said Martín the elder, son of a Dreamer, was to be sacrificed by the Aztecs in one of their secret cult rituals. And that his sacrificial death would signal the end of Spanish rule.

Martín the elder, who was more Spaniard than Mexican in his upbringing, who had only a residual memory of his mother and her customs, knew nothing of his supposed role in the religious aspirations of the Aztecs. Thus, his torture produced no confessions, and the winds are still pregnant with his denials—"For the love of God, I can't tell you what I don't know!"

Still, the Spaniards, ever fearful of the power of Aztec witchcraft, exiled the elder Martín to the Old World to ensure that his ritual death would not take place. But it was all to no effect.

Many years later, Martín would die in the company of a Moorish sorcerer and alchemist. The Moor had Martín's burnt bones transported to Mexico by Portuguese mariners in exchange

for maps that supposedly revealed the secret location of the fountain of youth. The Portuguese delivered the remains to one of the Moor's accomplices in the brotherhood of alchemists, a Jesuit monk, who was later apprehended and executed by the office of the Inquisition. But before his arrest, the monk, who had learned to decipher the picture language of the Aztecs and knew of their religious philosophies, buried Martín's remains in a secret place to await the fruition of the Indian prophecies. And so, from that time until the promised return of the multilingual woman, the spirit of Martín Cortés would haunt the dreams of Indians and Spaniards alike.

3

Gathering of Omens

In the metropolis of modern Mexico City, the one who would discover Malintzín's new identity was a one hundred and twenty-four year old Indian healer named *Doña* Regina Delgado, also called La Nahua because she spoke the old Mexican language, Nahuatl. The eldest and most superstitious neighbors in her *colonia* on the outskirts of Mexico City said La Nahua was old enough to remember the conquest, confusing her with her great-grandmother who was also called Regina. They would say, "She must be five hundred years old because she was old when I was a child."

Every morning La Nahua was seen returning to the colonia from the city with a knapsack.

"What do you have there, *Doña* Regina?" her neighbors would ask.

"Omens," La Nahua would say, and she would show them the contents of her knapsack: discarded roses, pieces of metal, bottle caps, chips of broken cobblestones, crumpled envelopes.

"What are you going to do with them?" they would ask derisively, because the significance of their dreams, if remembered at all, was drowned out by the brutish forces of their poverty.

La Nahua, always inscrutable and beyond offense, would say, "When I gather enough signs, I will be able to find Malintzín and know for certain when the world of my people will begin again."

When La Nahua was out of earshot, the neighbors would always say, "Crazy old woman." And they would go about their lives.

One morning, La Nahua went to the Basilica Of Guadalupe to pray and, in the courtyard, stumbled upon a note.

The note said:

> *Querida* María Elena,
>
> I love you, and I will find you again. Somehow, this letter will reach you.
>
> *El que sueña contigo,*
>
> Sebastian.

"So that is her name!" exclaimed La Nahua out loud. "María Elena."

La Nahua remembered what her great-grandmother had told her, that when the world was nearing its end, letters would lose their way to their intended owners. She was certain this particular letter was meant for Malintzín. 'The one who wrote the letter sent it here because this is where he supposed she would be,' she thought. 'The spirit of Martín Cortés must also be nearby. Regina la grande, my great-grandmother, said it would be.'

That night, La Nahua had a portentous dream. She dreamt that an earthquake convulsed the ceremonial temple center in Uxmal, releasing the spirit of Martín Cortés. The next day, she boarded a bus and went to the ruins of Teotihuacán outside of Mexico City. La Nahua had never tried to reason her way through a sign, but let it take its own form, let it create its own meaning. There in Teotihuacán, whose name signifies 'the city of the gods,' she waited for the spirit of Martín Cortés, or another lost letter, or the narratives embedded in the frequencies of the winds, or perhaps even Malintzín herself.

With the exception of a policeman, no one took special note of La Nahua, thinking her to be just another old Indian woman come to beg. After a long time, the policeman approached La Nahua, who sat on the steps of the Pyramid of the Moon, entranced in her inner waking dreams. When he asked her if she was waiting for someone, she responded, "I am listening to the voices in the wind."

4

Malintzín

The wise men of the ancient Aztec world, who had learned the art of astronomy and the divination of time from the Toltecs before them, who in turn had learned it from the Olmecs and Teotihua-cános before them, knew that all worlds must die and be reborn, that all things that happen once, repeat fatalistically in the mysterious cycles of time. Their calendars documented the birth and death of the Five Suns or the Five Epochs. But the prophecies called for another end of the world. The year that marked the end was *Ce Acatl*, when the exiled, bearded, white god, Quetzalcoatl, would return.

But, unknown to them, the end had been launched years before, beginning with the birth of a woman, Malintzín, the daughter of an Aztec nobleman. While she was still in her mother's womb, her parents consulted a fortune teller to divine the fate of their child. The fortune teller said the baby's birth would coincide with the prophesied onset of evil omens. "This child will bring an end to the world."

After the birth of Malintzín, her father died and her

mother remarried. Perhaps out of fear for the fortune teller's prophecies, or perhaps because the mother and step-father wished to secure their newborn son's place as sole heir, Malintzín was sold into slavery. She remained a slave until she was a young woman, highly valued because of her extraordinary ability—she was multilingual, speaking the languages of the Aztecs and the Mayas alike—and because of her beauty and the serenity of her character. She was also rumored to have given birth to a child by her Aztec master.

More important, however, to the rulers, *caciques*, of her region, Malintzín was a Dreamer, a magician who could interpret omens from the wells of sleep. Few possessed this ability, and most were important men in the courts of the Aztec princes or the emperor Moctezuma. The people of Malintzín's town first discovered she could read their dreams when, as a young child, she told her masters, "I saw myself being dreamed." And she went on to describe, one by one, the dreams of the members of her master's household. With her divining gifts accepted and encouraged, she rapidly learned the secret language of dreams.

At the beginning of her menses, Malintzín began to hear voices embedded in the lower frequencies of the wind. She began to gather the lost conversations of the winds and the fragments of dreams she found there. Some of the images and lost voices were those of the dead, but most pertained to the future. Gradually, the evil omens that had begun to appear since the time of her childhood began to coalesce into a single ominous prophecy: the end of the Aztec world.

The coming of these evil omens filled the people with dread, and a contagion of insomnia afflicted many people. The first signs were a drought and a terrible food shortage. The following year, lightening struck a temple in the center of Tenochtitlán. A few years later, a cone of light appeared in the sky. One day the sun showered the skies with fire, causing a temple to burst into flames and the waters of Lake Texcoco to boil.

But in the face of the anxieties of common folk and magicians alike, Malintzín remained calm, secure in her conviction that the events were not foreshadowing merely death, but the advent of a new creation. In numerous dream-visions, she saw the future beyond the destruction of the world. Malintzín dreamed herself as the nexus of a new beginning, the mother of a new race, and she saw the old gods and rituals melt into the secret chambers of women's wombs, hibernating through the centuries, the old world remembered in the dementia of dreams, the poetry of the land sung in a strange new language. She saw the nation of her future children transformed into new men, filled with the memories of distant rivers, visions of a remote, sunlit land of high mountains and stone palaces. Malintzín dreamed of her people's people, epochs before, seeking refuge from voracious glaciers, separated from other men who were pale skinned, only to be reunited with these men, to again mix their blood. So she waited patiently, like a bird anticipating the sunrise.

The calm of Malintzín contrasted sharply to the anxieties of the Aztec emperor Moctezuma. As the omens increased, so did his efforts to please the gods through religious penitence. In the time of Moctezuma's great-grandfather, the magicians had, similarly, predicted that the world would end with a terrible earthquake. His forefathers had averted that disaster by increased human sacrifices. Moctezuma followed that example and ordered more young warriors from Tlaxcala be captured and sacrificed.

And so it was, like a great fountain, blood flowed from the great temple of Huitzilopochtli and the air was pregnant with the metallic smell of blood. One night, Moctezuma, lost in the mercury of his insomnia, heard a woman weeping by the causeways. "Oh, my children! They are lost!" Terrified, he ordered the royal guard to find the woman, but they could not because, they said, she seemed to be everywhere at once and no place in particular.

Soon thereafter, the fishermen of Lake Texcoco found a mysterious gray bird that resembled a crane, with a round diadem set in its forehead. Finally, the men of the city captured a strange creature with two heads that was like two men squeezed together, but it vanished before it could be seen by the emperor.

Disturbed by these apparitions, Moctezuma gathered the greatest Dreamers of the empire and had them interpret the signs. They told Moctezuma, "The weeping woman is a phantom from another time. She mourns for your destroyed kingdom."

Angered by the divinations of the Dreamers, Moctezuma ordered their execution. But the omens and signs continued because, unknown to Moctezuma, the most powerful Dreamer had escaped the slaughter. Malintzín, woman and slave. Perhaps if she had also died then, the prophecies would have lost their way like a ship without a beacon, and the Aztecs would have been saved. But that was not to be.

From the eastern outskirts of the Aztec empire, came the news of temples in the sea. The beings from the temples, as if to assert their divinity, had weapons that would breathe fire and stones. Then the most fearful of news came. The beings were in the likeness of men, but with pale skin and feathers on their faces. At their command were large 'deer,' and when these white-feathered beings mounted the 'deer,' they became one with the animals.

"It can be no one other than Quetzalcoatl," said the Aztecs, for this was the Year *Ce Acatl*, the year of our Lord, 1519.

Moctezuma sent his ambassadors to meet the pale-skinned gods with feathers on their faces. When the ambassadors returned, they reported to the emperor the gods' displeasure with their offerings, how the gods reacted with violent disgust at their sacrifice of a young warrior, and how the one called Hernán Cortés, the leader of these gods, had them—the ambassadors—chained and forced to witness the firing of a monstrous weapon that roared like thunder.

The ambassadors also told Moctezuma that his subjects in Tabasco had given Cortés a young woman named Malintzín to serve as his interpreter. They did not tell Moctezuma that Malintzín had conveyed a secret message to him. She had told the ambassadors, "Tell the emperor and the people to heed the message that our wise men have been repeating: There is a god greater than our many gods and that he is the creator of all things. These beings from the east are not gods, but mere men. They also know of this god. This creator must be great to be known by so many in different lands. I have heard it spoken in the wind currents and in the language of dreams that if we accept this god, our world will be reborn, that the mother goddess Tonantzín will come clothed in the vestments of the old world and the new."

However, for probably no other reason than that she was a woman, the ambassadors did not heed or relay her message. If they had listened to Malintzín, and conveyed her message to Moctezuma, the Aztecs might have been spared the utter brutality of the horrific conquest that followed. But that, also, was not to be.

After the conquest, Malintzín was seen weeping by the causeways. Some said it was because she had been abandoned by her lover, Hernán Cortés, who had departed to the eastern sea, taking their son, Martín with him. But those laments were not for herself, but for the destroyed cities. She had no romantic illusions about Cortés. She knew he was using her just as she had been used by the men of her own people. Malintzín wept because she felt betrayed by what had become her true love: the Christian god. She had not imagined that the Church of her new god would consecrate the acts of the conquerors who, although they had given her freedom and a legal husband, the Spanish gentleman and con- quistador Juan Jamarillo, had left her world awash in ashes and blood, rotting bones among broken stones, infants weeping over the corpses of their mothers. But while the military conquest may have obliterated the In- dian regimes, it was the Dominican friars of the Church, warriors of the Cross, who ultimately crushed the spirit of the ancient Mexicans.

The Indians were accustomed to the ritual violence of human sacrifice, but these had been restricted to a select class of individuals: warriors, and noblemen and noblewomen. They were, thus, unprepared for the ferocity of the friars, emboldened by the Church- sanctioned Inquisition, whose religious fervor had escalated to a form of spiritual terrorism against all men, noble and common alike. The robed and stern- faced Dominicans and their macabre machinery of tor- ture soon cowed the surviving populace into submis- sion. The Churchmen, in spectacular bonfires, burned the books of the Aztecs, exiling their memories to the winds that devoured the smoke.

Soon thereafter, Malintzín, her son, Martín, gone for- ever, died from one of the diseases of the white men. But those who could see, those remaining Dreamers who had the power, said her weeping spirit continued to roam at night, wandering the streets and causeways of Mexico City as if in self-imposed exile from heaven.

And thus, the defeated Aztecs said of Malintzín, "She will come again."

"She has gone to learn the language and secrets of the gods. When she returns, our world will begin again."

"We must look for the return of the woman of many tongues."

Those who could not read the meanings in their dreams asked the wise men and sorcerers, "What will be the other signs?"

The wise men and sorcerers said, "These: a great earthquake and the appearance of Iberians fleeing a war. Also these: a contagion of insomnia, the voices of the dead heard in the winds, a prophetic dream of a land with three moons. There will also be sightings of the Cholulan priests, their faces painted green and white, and written messages that lose their way to their intended owner. And, finally, we shall witness the return of Martín Cortés."

5

Malediction of the Hours

Silvia Vázquez was deep in thought, still grieving for her husband José who had died months earlier, when she received the news of María Elena's accident. She was sitting alone in her garden at her home near downtown San José. The large trees that surrounded her home muffled the noise of the nearby city. A Moorish-style water fountain gurgled rhythmically, enticing her further into her sanctuary of memory. In her solitary trance, she recreated the events of the past in exacting details although her thoughts were occasionally interrupted by the beauty of the flowers which the resplendent California sun seemed to illuminate like phosphorescent jewels.

"*Señora* Vázquez?" The dark, funereal tone of the male voice calling from Mexico caused Silvia's stomach to compress as when riding a rollercoaster.

"Yes, this is Silvia Vázquez."

"We regret to inform you, *Señora*, that the archeological site your daughter, María Elena, was excavating collapsed during yesterday's earthquake. Your daughter is missing, but we have implemented emergency measures. . . ."

She did not hear the rest of the message, instead she again recalled the vague superstitions of Sephardic ancestors: 'A curse shall pass from father to son, unto the seventh generation.'

Silvia had first heard those words spoken by her great-grandfather Ezequiel Treviño a day before his death. Silvia was but nine years old, and because she was terrified by the convictions of the old man, she became deeply religious. Since that time, she had never missed a single Sunday mass, nor neglected her devotional duties on days of obligation. Her piety had helped bury her fears, and like the rest of her people, she not only did not dwell on her Spanish Hebraic origins, but had acquired a sense of security in the Catholic faith her forefathers had reluctantly adopted.

The only other time Silvia remembered the superstition of her ancestors was when her nephew Sebastian, after twenty years of fascination with the magical arts of his maternal grandfather Pedro Eloy Joaquín, fell into a spell of perpetual hallucinations. Having loved her nephew as her own son, she refused to have him institutionalized and had him brought to her home where she cared for him.

'They say they everything happens in twos,' She thought as she fearfully pondered the latest disaster. 'If it is so, it is not fair, for at least my nephew has lived half of his life, and, God be merciful!, he may still recover. But María Elena! Poor *Mi hija* is not even twenty-six and perhaps she is already dead.'

Later that evening, as her children Ricardo, Josesito,

and Rachel were making preparations to leave for Mexico, Silvia, preoccupied by her memories, said to them, "Perhaps there was a curse on your father's people. Your grandfather Gustavo used to talk about a ghost that haunted his village in Extremadura."

"That is nonsense, *Mamá*," said Ricardo, who had always dismissed stories of his grandfather Gustavo Vázquez as senile rantings.

As the eldest of Silvia's children, Ricardo had assumed the role of family head with brusque efficiency, and earlier had nixed the plans of his own children, nieces and nephews to go with them to Mexico. "Only four people are needed to bring back the corpse," said Ricardo, which instead of preparing the young people for the worst scenario, merely incited them to uncontrollable crying.

Offended by their emotional outburst, he ordered them to cease their weeping. "You must be strong. You are all too old to be acting like children. Besides, your grandmother Silvia needs you to care for your uncle Sebastian."

During the flight from San Francisco to the Yucatán, the four hardly spoke, each lost in his or her own thoughts and mortifications. Silvia silently prayed the rosary, occasionally glancing at the faces of her children. Her sons remained stoic, refusing food, consuming nothing but ice water.

'Ah, they still renounce God!' thought Silvia bitterly. 'Just like their father.'

While her husband was gravely ill, hoping for a deathbed conversion, she had asked a priest to come and administer the Last Rites. True to his atheist beliefs which he had cultivated in his youth as a university student in Madrid, José refused. And smiling ironically, pronounced, "There is no God."

Turning her thoughts away from her husband, she looked at her daughter, Rachel, who tried her best to emulate the stoicism of her brothers. Instead she kept wiping away tears and suppressing sighs. José had never made exceptions for Rachel's sensitive nature and expected the same stoicism that came so easily to Ricardo and Josesito. Rachel, in her futile attempts to please her father, barricaded her emotions behind an aloofness than many times gave her the air of arrogance, which people assumed was a result of vanity associated with beauty. Behind her back, the family's neighbors and friends would say of Rachel, *"Presumida!* She thinks because she is well-off and has beauty that she is never going to grow old or be miserable!"

'Poor, *mi hija,* no one knows how she suffers,' thought Silvia between Hail Marys . 'The humiliations that we have hid for her sake. Perhaps if José had let her pay for her mistakes long ago, she would not have to endure this tragedy in her prison of silence.'

Silvia's stream of thoughts were interrupted by her memory of the voice of Ezequiel Treviño, almost as if it had been evoked from the cyclical hum of the jet engines. "A curse . . . from generation to generation. . . . "

6

María Elena

N ever in the recent collective memory of the Maya were they able to recall an earthquake like the one that convulsed the ceremonial center in the ancient city of Uxmal. The Maya had not witnessed an earthquake for generations, but even in their oral histories there was nothing that resembled this one: for when the earth trembled, it emanated a loud roar like that of a wounded jaguar. Fortunately, the earthquake occurred early in the morning, when, with the exception of the archeologists and their assistants, the ruins were devoid of people. Among those present, only one was seriously injured: María Elena Vázquez, a member of the State University of Pennsylvania's archeological team.

María Elena was excavating a previously undiscovered burial site inside the Pyramid of the Magician. She had been retained by the university after her graduate work was completed and assigned to the region because of her superior scholarship and her multilingual abilities. She had discovered the burial site based on her informal but numerous conversations with the Indians of the region, of whom she had a vast network. She had assembled them through her frequent invitations to accompany other archeologists—not only from her own team, but from France and Britain as well—to serve as their translator. She was one of the select few who could speak several dialects of Mayan and Nahuatl. Even if she did not know a dialect, it was said, she had the extraordinary ability to decipher it, seemingly by breathing in the same space as the native speakers. The people in her archeological circle affectionately nicknamed her '*Doña* Marina'—the Christian name of the Spanish conqueror Hernán Cortés's interpreter.

By the time the rescue team extricated María Elena from the rubble of the collapsed excavation site, three days after the earthquake, her capacity for coherent language had been lost. At first, no one realized that she had been robbed of her many languages. When they first found her she was still unconscious, suffering from a severe concussion and dehydration. However, after she regained consciousness, her first attempts at communicating produced a incomprehensible language filled with the musical cadences of the Indian dialects. Those who first heard her speak were the swing shift doctor at the hospital in Mérida and her Maya field assistant Tanilo Tun and his wife Elsie who had come to bring her some flowers. The doctor merely assumed that she was speaking Mayan to her friends, but Tanilo and Elsie Tun knew otherwise. Not only was she not speaking Mayan, she was not speaking Nahuatl either, for they had heard her use that language before and this one was very different.

By the time her family and doctors came to understand the true nature of her problem, the news of María Elena's strange language had been spread by her two friends in the town and in the marketplace in Mérida. The people who heard the news in Mérida spread it to other marketplaces and the towns and hamlet from which they came. Days later, whenever the story was recounted, some said that a spirit, released from the bowels of the pyramid by the earthquake, had stolen María Elena Vázquez's languages and given her a new, unintelligible idiom.

At the hospital in Mérida, her fiancé, Manuel Muñoz, a corporate bank attorney from Mexico City, and her family who had flown in from California, were constantly at her bedside. The hospital corridors were also usually crowded with the popular young archeologist's friends, colleagues and the common folk of the surrounding villages. Much to everyone's relief, María Elena suffered from no life-threatening injuries and quickly recovered. Even her inability to communicate did not especially alarm her doctors, colleagues and family, as all were safe in the assumption that she was speaking an Indian language. However, it didn't take long for María Elena to realize that she was not being understood and she quickly became agitated, speaking more rapidly, and punctuating her ramblings with the name, "Sebastian," the name of her cousin and adopted brother. Her frustration and agitation were met with misplaced sympathy, as everyone assumed she was suffering from emotional trauma. That assumption lasted for several days—until the return of María Elena's friends, Tanilo Tun and his wife, Elsie.

"She is not speaking our language," said Tanilo Tun.

"But there are many dialects of your language," said Silvia Vázquez. "How can you be so certain?"

"The language that your daughter is speaking is buried with the tongues of the dead," interjected Elsie Tun.

"Nonsense!" said Manuel Muñoz, a young man filled with modern ideas, and who, like many of the Mexican higher classes, held an overt disdain for the Indians and their ancient customs. "Take your stupid superstitions out of here!" he added.

But María Elena took her friend Elsie's hand as if to rebuff her fiancé.

"Careful, friend," Ricardo warned Manuel upon seeing her gesture. "These people have their own ways. Their customs may be different from ours, but my sister has great love and respect for them."

"Yes," seconded Josesito. "If you truly love our sister, you'll respect her friends."

Those remarks silenced Manuel Muñoz, but at the same time deepened his resentment towards the Vázquez brothers. Manuel knew that they, too, had no stomach for superstitions. The brothers' remarks were, in fact, a rebuke and rejection of Manuel, who they had never liked. They regarded his positions on politics and economics undemocratic and socially unjust. Like their father and grandfather before them, all of the Vázquez family, including María Elena, were passionate liberals. What irritated Manuel, however, was that their liberalism did not extend to family interactions. Instead, they adhered to the traditional, conservative Hispanic honor codes, with the men of the family holding the sway of benevolent patriarchs. They resented his romance with María Elena because she had already given herself to him.

After their reprimand, Manuel remained silent. It was Rachel Vázquez, unnerved by the length of the silence, who finally changed the subject. "*Señora* Tun?" she asked María Elena's friend. "Why do you say such a thing?"

It was the first time Rachel Vázquez had spoken in the presence of anyone but her family and doctors. Startled, Tanilo and Elsie Tun stared at the middle-aged woman, as if noticing her for the first time. Their stares made Rachel visibly uneasy. "Well?" she insisted.

"María Elena's many languages were stolen, and she was given the idiom of the dead instead," said Elsie.

"Yes," said Tanilo. "The one who took her languages will come again and try to find her. He has been looking for her for a while."

"Who?" asked Rachel Vázquez. "Who is coming for her?"

"Martín Cortés," responded Tanilo. "He is a spirit—"

"I've had enough!" exploded Ricardo Vázquez. And in a rare moment of unity between the two men, Ricardo Vázquez and Manuel Muñoz demanded that María Elena be examined by a psychiatrist.

María Elena underwent a battery of psychiatric tests. At the behest of her former professor, who was convinced that María Elena was speaking a dialect of Athapaskan,

which was one of her languages, she was also inter-
viewed by two linguists friends of his from Britain. The
psychiatrist concluded that her strange language was a
symptom of the trauma she suffered from her accident.
The linguists' finding were more intriguing, although
frightful to María Elena's family. As far as the linguists
could discern, María Elena was speaking an Asiatic language—the roots of some of the words were similar to
some of the Siberian dialects, but the inflections and the
syntax were archaic or altogether obscure. Despite a me-
ticulous compilation of María Elena's new language, the
linguists could find no match in their databases.

Elsie Tun, who had henceforth returned every day to
be at her friend's side and had heard the linguists'
analysis, offered her own interpretation. "The two
gentlemen cannot make sense of María Elena's language
because she is dreaming awake."

Elsie then showed the linguists drawings María
Elena had made since she regained consciousness. The
drawings appeared to be written in an iconographic inscription. One of the linguists, who had his undergradu-
ate degree in civil engineering remarked, "If I didn't
know better, I'd swear these were some kind of schematics or perhaps—this is very strange—these could be
maps." He then noted some of the mathematical and
cartographic elements.

Fascinated by their findings, the two linguists
wanted to conduct a study, but Manuel Muñoz refused
to cooperate and ordered them to leave.

When María Elena left the hospital, Manuel Muñoz
took her home with him to Mexico City. "She's going to

be my wife, so I will care for her," he insisted over her family's objections. He took a month's leave of absence from his job, and devoted himself to making her the same woman who had loved him so well and supported his dreams. María Elena proved easy to care for, since she had no ailment other than her language deficiency, and she could understand the speech of others, read, and participate in life. Soon, she and Manuel were living a routine that could be described as normal: they went for walks in Chapultepec Park, and they visited the museums, movie theaters, coffee houses, and clubs. Manuel, who was always jealous of sharing her with her archeology friends, took the liberty of limiting the number and duration of their visits. María Elena's Indian friends, intimidated by Manuel's open hostility towards them, stayed away. Manuel also took care not to expose his friends to María Elena after he heard one make a casual but revealing remark about her.

"I heard from one of her associates at the museum that her brother Sebastian's delusional. Maybe there's insanity in their blood," said Manuel's friend.

Manuel Muñoz understood his society, *"la sociedad"* as it is referred to by the Mexicans—the other upper-class power players like himself—very well. His was a tight knit network, and if one friend was thinking that his fiancée was crazy, they would all come to the same conclusion. Manuel could not have imagined what they were thinking about him.

"Manuelito always wanted to dominate that girl— she's always been the independent sort—and now he's got his chance."

But he was quickly becoming oblivious to the opinion of his peers and to the thing he had lived for: the desire for power. His basic nature had been affected because, a chronic insomniac, he suddenly found that he could sleep the entire night. Since adolescence, when he first became afflicted with insomnia, he had rested only in short naps during the day, and spent the reminder of his waking hours working, giving him an edge over his competitors at school and, later, in his profession. But now, María Elena's presence and her constant dreaming lured him into the rivers of sleep. Much to his surprise, he, too, found himself dreaming.

At first, the dreams were pleasant, even benevolently forgettable. Then, after a few days of sleeping, he began to dream of grotesque scenarios. He dreamed of being chased in a tropical rain forest by a group of Indian sorcerers who had their faces painted green and white. At other times, he dreamed that he was watching María Elena's eyes, but it was not she, but a man with a scarred face who was performing a secret ritual at an abandoned Indian ruin. Many times, he saw a green-eyed man and the sorcerers pursuing him until the earth began to convulse, open up, and devour him. Horrified, he forced himself to give up the pleasure of sleep.

One evening, he opened the door to the terrace of his house to let in the night winds. He went back inside and turned on his computer. He was reading his e-mail when he heard a man's voice in a murmuring undertone. Manuel withdrew a pistol he kept in his drawer and said in a loud voice, "Who's there?" The voice seemed to move away, back towards the opened door.

He went out on the terrace, thinking some passerby was mocking him, and shouted into the street, "Who goes there?" But no one responded. 'I must be losing my mind,' he told himself, and agitated, went into the bedroom to lie down next to María Elena.

She was in a deep sleep, but unlike the other nights, she was talking in her Asiatic language, punctuating her monologue with the name "Sebastian." Manuel listened to her talk, as if for a singular moment she would magically begin to speak in Spanish and reveal her secrets to him. There were many things, he remembered, she had been evasive about, concealing, even in their most intimate moments, her deepest identity, as if to tell him that he could not possess her.

María Elena continued to speak, as if to the very wind, until the rains finally came and drowned out her desire to communicate. Early in the morning, while it was still dark, another windstorm blew through the city. When the wind rushed through the house, Manuel again heard the low, murmuring male voice. Manuel thought he could make out what the voice said: "My grandfather's become a coyote." Then María Elena began talking in her sleep again. Filled with inexplicable jealously, Manuel brusquely shook her out of her dreams.

"Wake up!" he said desperately. He noticed her eyes were like a murky green ocean. Inexplicably, she began to weep.

"What's wrong?" he asked angrily. "What are you thinking about?"

Unlike other times when she would try to speak to

him in her Asiatic language, she turned her back and continued to weep.

Filled with feelings of betrayal and alienation, Manuel got dressed and left the house, and drove to the *Zócalo* to go for a walk. During his many years of insomnious vigils, he had taken to walking the *Zócalo* at night. His mother, ever fearful of the criminals and transients who roamed the dark, had begged him not to persist with his habit. Even Manuel's father, who believed that a man had absolute freedom, found himself agreeing with his wife and asked his son not to walk the *Zócalo* at night. The gigantic plaza was at this time filled with many Indians who had come from the countryside to protest against the government (when the Indians' demands were shrugged off by the government, they had set up a tent city in the huge plaza).

But Manuel, armed with his pistol, feared nothing. In fact, his attitude and demeanor telegraphed a death challenge, daring anyone to confront him. He would look the other passersby in the eyes, and unconsciously flex his muscular fists. The men he met would look away, conceding he had power over them. But the women and children who peered at him through the tents like passive rabbits, blankly fixed their eyes on Manuel more in a gesture of resignation than fear.

As he walked, Manuel lapsed into deep introspection, analyzing his romance with María Elena, how she, unlike the other women in his life, had met his advances with utter indifference.

When he first met María Elena Vázquez at a benefit dinner for the National Museum of Anthropology in

Mexico City, he was already engaged to another woman, but the young archeologist and her mysterious beauty immediately obsessed him. The investment bank he worked for had asked him to go to the dinner to accompany a wealthy client from the United States whose true passion was collecting pre-Columbian artifacts and Spanish colonial manuscripts. Manuel spotted María Elena among a group of her friends and colleagues, who, by their animated gestures and laughter, were engaged in some humorous storytelling. Whenever she spoke, she tossed her hair about and momentarily looked skyward, as if plucking the memories from the air. Seeming to feel his watchful eyes, she turned and looked at him, still possessed of the smile she reserved for her friends. He remembered that she held her gaze just long enough to acknowledge him, and still smiling, returned her attention to her beloved friends. She would have relegated him to her stores of forgetfulness had he not made a point to not only introduce himself that evening, but, a few days later, to come by the archeological lab where she worked.

After those initial meetings, he wanted only to have her, but later he wanted her to love him. Within a month of meeting María Elena, he broke off his engagement and, to the annoyance of María Elena's friends, relentlessly pursued his new obsession. Much to his frustration, only part of her work was done in her office in Mexico City. Most of the time, if she was not with her field team from the university at their site in the Yucatán, she was with another team serving as their translator. He literally pursued her around the country, determined to breakdown her indifference towards him.

Manuel rehashed these memories as he circled the huge plaza, repeatedly passing an old priest, who was engaged in his own insomniac introspections. The following night and several nights thereafter, Manuel returned to the *Zócalo* to walk and think, leaving María Elena alone in the company of her dreams. He encountered the same priest every night, but Manuel, who disdained the church and its teachings—he considered the church an institution of ignorance and its priests emasculated hypocrites—did not recognize this accidental, nocturnal companion as the same one he had previously encountered. Only once did the priest catch Manuel's attention, because as they passed each other, Manuel thought he heard the priest speak to him.

"Infidel, filled with power and fornication," murmured a masculine voice.

Manuel reversed course and belligerently came upon the priest. "What did you say to me, *Señor?*"

The priest recognized the threatening tone, but was not afraid of the young man. "I have said nothing," he responded firmly and resumed walking.

Manuel thought, 'That one is a real man.' The priest turned around and looked at the young man, as if he had heard Manuel's secret thought.

When Manuel returned home after his encounter with the priest, he found María Elena sitting on the terrace, speaking into the winds.

". . . Sebastian. . . ."

" . . . "

"Sebastian. . . ."

Something in the vocal quality of her voice disturbed him. Her tone was secretive, filled with gentle illicitness. Manuel had never heard her speak in that tone of voice, and he was again filled with inexplicable jealousy. He had to find an explanation for her behavior. 'I cannot go on like this,' he told himself.

At wit's end, he decided to arrange for his sister to care for María Elena while he took the earliest possible flight to California. He hoped her family would be able to tell him something of María Elena's past that would help explain her mental ailment.

7

The Priest

Upon completing his night-long walk, Father Fernando Ocampo returned to the Cathedral and reported directly for his duty shift without breakfast. He was too agitated to think of food even though he had walked the entire night, remembering the young man he had encountered in the *Zócalo*.

'He heard me thinking,' mused Father Fernando of Manuel Muñoz, although he did not know that was the young man's name.

The priest was accustomed to hearing voices—he had been hearing them for sixty-four years, since his novitiate in Querétaro. He had always assumed the voices were those of the restless and unrepentant dead, but this episode in the *Zócalo* was the first time he had experienced another seeming to hear his thoughts. Filled with the confusion of wakefulness and the electricity of his encounter, Father Fernando went to hear early confessions.

As he walked to the confessional, Father Fernando Ocampo was filled with the same chill he had experienced every day since his arrival in Mexico City, as if the

Baroque stone and the serpentine inlaid gold of the Cathedral were concealing a Paleolithic glacier. His eyes met the vacuous eyes of the statutes of the saints whose pathetic stares were like those of worm-eaten skulls. The cavernous Cathedral was empty except for the most hopeless and the oldest of believers who knelt in the pews and prayed silently. When Father Fernando entered the confessional, he expected to find an old penitent, not a youthful, melancholic sinner.

"Because it is not a sin, Father," said a young woman's voice that seemed to the sleep deprived priest to be filled with the melodies of dreams.

"What is not a sin?" asked Father Fernando, perplexed that she did not begin her confession in the prescribed manner.

"What you call sin, Father, should be called love," she responded. "Is it true, Father, that our Lord Jesus said, 'How can you claim to love God whom you cannot see, and not love your brother whom you can see?'"

"Not in those exact words. Our Lord said, . . ." Father Fernando stopped because his eyes had adjusted to the darkness, and he saw that the confessional was empty. He quickly stepped out to see if he could catch a glimpse of the sinner, but there was no one in the Cathedral except those he had seen before.

"Perhaps it was another ghost," said Fernando to himself in resignation.

Fernando Ocampo was tired, not only because he had spent the last several nights walking, and worse, encountering the same young man in the *Zócalo* who was filled with violent thoughts—yes, Fernando now realized that he, too, was reading the other's mind—but because the voices of the night had become more prevalent than ever, as if they were foreshadowing a calamity or a wonder. His gift for deciphering the voices of the night, which many years ago Fernando interpreted to be a divine grant—"So that I can best understand the hearts of men," he had thought—now seemed to him a punishment. In his old age he had prayed for the voices to be silenced, or at the very least to be replaced by those of angels. Instead, the darkest of sinners followed him more than ever.

When Fernando Ocampo entered the seminary, Mexico had just ended its bloodiest revolution. During the war and in the years that followed, the revolutionaries relentlessly persecuted the Church and her sons, and many priests died by the rope or by firing squad. Despite the country's anti-cleric atmosphere, the young Fernando Ocampo rejected the secular zeal of the country's political liberalism for his own dreamer's fascinations with the mysteries of religion and antiquity. His passion for his studies and devotional duties so obsessed him that he became afflicted with severe insomnia. He spent entire nights reading the stories of the saints and martyrs—St. Lucy plucking out her eyes to preserve her chastity, St. Sebastian strewn with arrows, St. Laurence roasted on a gridiron. In the chaos of his imagination, he heard what he first thought to be water running down the stone walls. The sound of water then changed into the low, dark murmurs of human voices. Trying to make sense of this phenomenon, he began to walk all night, hoping that the mystery would offer some cohesive vision.

The abbot was not aware of Fernando Ocampo's predicament until one evening when he heard some shots fired in the town followed by the shouts of soldiers. The abbot opened the window and saw someone enter the monastery garden from the street. He ran to a window that faced the garden.

"Who goes there?" the abbot shouted from the window.

"I, Fernando Ocampo," said the young novice.

"Come back inside, son," called out the abbot. "The soldiers are hunting holy men again."

Once inside the abbey, Fernando was asked what he was doing walking at night.

"Listening to the voices of the dead, Father," said Fernando, and he went on to recount the secrets hidden in time and stone.

He related to the abbot and two other priests the stories spoken by the voices: how many years ago some of the most devout and respectable Christian families of Querétaro had sent their daughters to the convents to secretly bear the children of illicit unions; how the abbots of old had secretly buried the murdered rivals of their supporters in the very garden where he spent his insomnious nights. Fernando then went on to relate a secret that was guarded with the utmost security.

"Maximilian von Hapsburg left some jewelry in the care of the abbot in 1867," said Fernando. "His spirit comes every Thursday night to look for a ring that Carlota gave him on his birthday."

The abbot and his assistants were horrified not only by the veracity of his tales—'How could he have learned these things?' they wondered—but were equally concerned that if the officials of the revolution were to learn these things, there could be more retaliations against the Church. With this in mind, they sent Fernando to Mexico City to finish his novitiate, both as a reward for his devotions and so he could be treated for his insomnia and, what they termed, his 'delusions.'

In Mexico City, Fernando was given immediate medical attention and with drugs, he soon recovered some of his sleeping habits. But he continued to hear voices, this time in the Cathedral of Mexico. What he heard in those sixty-four years were mere fragments of conversations and bitter complaints, but nothing like voices that followed him now. They crowded his mind and competed fiercely for his attention, seeking absolution from the realm of the dead. The noise gave him terrible migraine headaches, and Fernando resumed the habit of his youth and returned to the streets at night, as if walking were sleeping, seeking refuge from the lost sinners.

The evening after Manuel Muñoz had heard his thoughts, Fernando Ocampo decided not to take his nocturnal walk. Instead, he retired to his room after a bath and tried to read and rest, but found he could not concentrate on his book as his mind kept drifting back to the strange events of the last several days. As if his memories were liquid currents, he suddenly remembered another bizarre confession he had heard nearly ten years before, which oddly seemed somehow related to the one he had heard that day because then, too, the confessional had been empty.

"I am a young man," the penitent had said.

"Is that your confession, son?"

"Yes."

"Youth is not a sin," Fernando recalled saying.

"God forgives only the old," persisted the penitent.

"Why do you say that, son?"

"Because the old are too tired to sin, Father."

Fernando woke from his drifting memory trance. He went to his closet and took out an old kerosene lamp he had brought from Querétaro sixty-four years before. He lit the lamp, turned off the electric lights, and opened his window to let in the night winds which held the promise of another rainstorm. Hours passed, and Fernando, lulled by the aroma of the burning kerosene into a state of semi-wakefulness, began to see a vision grow out of the flames. It seemed like a dream, but it was filled with the sensations of reality, as if he had been transported to another place where things were called by different names. From the red and orange of the flames the figure of a young woman slowly coalesced. She spoke to Fernando in a strange language and beckoned him to follow her. He tried to resist her, but was unable to escape the lure of her green eyes which were like the restless sea. He followed her, lethargic and robotic, as if obeying some unseen, but greater force. Fernando heard a man's voice call out to him from the mists of the shadows.

"Are you of the living or the dead, Father?"

"The living," said Fernando. "And you, son?"

"The same, Father," responded the man.

Fernando felt the world of mists convulse, as if he were floating upon water.

"It is another storm," said the man. "You do not get seasick, do you Father?"

"Yes, can you make it stop?"

"Only she can make it stop, Father, but he has taken her prisoner as he has me."

"Who are you talking about? Who took you prisoner?"

"The sorcerer captain. He is the ruler of this world of inverse geometries, and he is insane. Be careful, Father, that he does not capture you as well."

"Who is this man, son?"

"A spirit. But he was once a man called Martín Cortés," said the man. And he shouted into the mists, "Vengeful phantom! I will not give you my eagle's secrets until you release my beloved!" And to Fernando, with tenderness, "Father, come closer where I can see you. I have been very lonely since she was taken away from me. And now her languages have been stolen!"

"Keep speaking, son, until I find you."

In his dream-vision, Fernando followed the man's voice until the wooden hull of an antiquated ship materialized from the mists. The man was perhaps in his early forties, lying naked on a cot, gravely ill from the motion of the sea. Fernando saw that the man's arms and legs were tattooed with inscrutable geometric patterns, and on his chest was the facsimile of an eagle.

"What you are looking at, Father, is the secret code of my eagle transformation. It was written on my body by my grandfather's people after my initiation into their visionary cults."

"What is your name?" asked Fernando.

"My grandfather's people call me Rising Eagle. The spirits, demons, or whatever they are of this boat call me the Mariner."

"And your Christian name, son?"

"Sebastian, after my mother's patron saint. . . . I'll not give the Sorcerer Captain my grandfather's secrets, Father. The Sorcerer Captain murdered my son and his namesake, killed the child while he was still in my beloved's womb. . . ."

Suddenly, the voice of Sebastian the Mariner became distorted, as if he were speaking through ice, and the vision dissolved as the sunlight entered Fernando's room.

Father Fernando, startled from his vision, became aware that he had not been conscious of his room, as if the night had passed without his having seen it. Instead, he thought, or at least his body felt, as if he had been awake the entire time but transported some where else. It was only then that Fernando Ocampo remembered what the old people of his town had told him years before when he was a child, that sometimes the voices of the night are not only those of the dead, but the secret thoughts and dreams of the living.

'Perhaps I was inside the mind of another,' thought Fernando. 'What if this man is real and needs my help?'

The following night, again unable to penetrate the

vapors of sleep, Father Fernando let himself be ruled by compassion and curiosity rather than the dogmas of the Church and its fear of the unknown. And he began to search for Sebastian the Mariner in the nocturnal chaos.

8

Sebastian

The night arrived accompanied by the intense throbbing of blood against Fernando Ocampo's temples. His ability to hear the frequencies of air and light aroused his senses to the point where he could discern the color of sound, or so he claimed. Many times in the past, the pain had been so intense that Father Fernando was hospitalized. During these extreme attacks, he experienced pain-induced visions during which he could see himself separated from his body, floating on air, the voices of his friends amplified as if they were machines rather than humans.

As soon as the pain began, Father Fernando, fearing the exaggerated symptoms of his migraines, went directly to bed. He pressed the palm of his hand against one throbbing temple and resisted the bitter, claustrophobic nausea that was growing in his stomach. He left the bedroom window open, hoping that the night voice of the mariner would return, but instead the sounds of the city—the roar of many engines, the excited shouts of night revelers, the dissonant turmoil of rock music—entered his bedroom. As his pain increased, the chaos of

those many sounds amplified and seemed to engulf him
as if an oily and evil phantom had penetrated his en-
trails and brain. Fernando pressed his palm more firmly
against his temple, slowing the desperate flow of his de-
mented blood. This time his attempts to ease the pain
worked, and his body began to fill with a sensation of
flight and dreaming. He listened to the sounds embedded in the secret chambers of the lower frequencies, and
he found again the one called Sebastian. Father
Fernando could not see him, but he could hear him
speaking, relating a tale, speaking in the intimate tones
of a spurned lover. Father Fernando heard him saying:

"I remember the first time I saw your father. I remember thinking, 'He is the great Indian Prince re-
born.' He could have been Cuauhtémoc escaped
from the prisons of time. Everything about him
was perfect: his warrior's physique, his black eyes,
the undaunted arrogance of royal Indian conquerors. Think, *querida*, what his people and yours
must have felt: the proud builders of a civilization
reduced to slavery, to the humiliation of servitude,
and the ravages of mysterious diseases. The only
way to persevere was through the silent memory of
genealogy. And with the patience of the stars, they
watched the passage of the centuries with feigned
indifference, so as to be re-born. . . . I saw him before she did, but it didn't matter because we both
loved him, in our own way.

"*Papá* José sent me with her because I was her
brother and men would respect her. That is what
the old man had said to me. "*Cuando hay un*

hombre, hay respecto." I was just a boy of sixteen, but of course I believed him, so did she. We all did except for Ricardo, but he was the oldest, and he had the freedom of a man. The rest of us were children, especially she and I. She because she was a woman, and I because I belonged to his dead brother, and I feared the spirits of my parents. We always obeyed, until later, that is. No, no, I meant to say until you . . . I can only see you in the most distant dream. I dreamt about you last night. You were little again and it was all right to love you. . . . When I finish this story, *querida,* use your many languages to find the secrets of my sleep death. It is the sickness of the ocean, *amor.* My liver is turning into ice. . . .

"The night when we met your father was her first dance and mine too. I had to get a false I.D. because they had a bar in the another part of the dance hall, but the old man said it didn't matter as if he were saying I could start doing men's things, but mostly I was there to protect her from the stares of men. He said, 'It is a father's curse to have a daughter of her beauty. You will understand, Sebastian, when you father such a daughter.'

"Although I was big for my age, it was obvious to the people at the dance hall that we were a couple of teenaged kids. But no one cared, and they let us in. Some guy who had once played with Augustín Lara had a band, and it was all like *Papá* José used to talk about, all the *muchachos* and *muchachas* dressed up in an elegant fantasy of the night. It seemed as if we were going to the same dances our parents went to, almost as if you could meet another generation of lovers who were trapped by a trick of time and who never left the room. I danced with her so that the men would know I was there and wouldn't try to get fresh with her. I wouldn't really know what love and its games were about until two years later when Ricardo took me to one of those cantinas in Tijuana. You always wanted to know what had happened, and I didn't ever want to tell you until now, perhaps because I've missed you so much. There was a woman who worked there who was Ricardo's friend. He said, "It's a coming of age gift, *manito*," and he told me to go with her. I remember being afraid, but I went along because I didn't want Ricardo to laugh at me. He didn't laugh at me the way Ramiro used to, but in a mean sort of way no one knew about except for Josesito and me.

"That night at my first dance, I asked Ramiro, 'What do you do, *carnal?*' and he laughed and said, 'I am the next Lightweight Champion of the world. And you, *güero?*' I said, 'I am my sister's protector.' Ramiro laughed again. 'I like you, *güero*. You are just a kid but you have balls. Who is your sister?' 'Her,' I said and I seemed to see her for the first time myself. She was so beautiful, just like you. I looked over at Ramiro and the way he looked at her was the way I would look at you, and we were both wrong for doing that . . . forget it, forget it, it's no use."

Sebastian's voice faded as the sun entered Father Fernando's room. Another night had passed, and Father Fernando, exhausted by sleeplessness and intoxicated by the euphoric relief he felt because the pain had eased completely, fell into a deep sleep.

9

Rachel

Manuel Muñoz arrived in San Francisco late in the evening and checked into a hotel near the airport. During his flight, Manuel decided that, contrary to good manners, he would not visit Silvia Vázquez or any other member of the family except for Rachel. He knew Silvia would never say anything remotely embarrassing about any member of her family. As for the two brothers, they would consider it an affront to their honor that he had even thought María Elena's problem was related to a family dysfunction.

On the other hand, his instincts told him Rachel might reveal some important detail, perhaps in an indirect manner. And her pride would prevent her from telling her brothers of his visit, which he wanted kept secret. He had discreetly observed Rachel during María Elena's hospitalization, and had noticed that Rachel subtly displayed powerful emotions which she masked behind her pride and sense of honor. Like María Elena, Rachel lapsed into moments of prolonged silence and feigned detachment, as if to deflect attention away from herself, hoping no one would confront her about her private thoughts. Manuel remembered how strangely Rachel had interacted with María Elena in front of her family, distant and reserved, showing only a formal sympathy that is usually given to strangers or enemies that one respects. But Manuel also had caught glimpses of repressed love beneath Rachel's silence and formality. He had seen those furtive emotions displayed in her eyes and in the clandestine caresses she gave María Elena.

'She is hiding something,' thought Manuel, knowing that the motivations for a lie always find a way of exposing themselves. And that was Rachel's trap, for in order to perpetuate her secret, she would, in her efforts to conceal it, expose something forbidden—whether it was a predisposition of habit or genetics—about the nature of María Elena's illness and perhaps the inner self that she constantly hid from him.

In the morning, he took a cab to downtown San Francisco where Rachel and her husband had their place of business. Although his trip was unexpected, Rachel nonetheless received him with a polite indifference, the same emotional projections that María Elena had also shown him on the night they first met. Rachel behaved towards him as if he were a professional associate rather than a future in-law. She took him on tour of her company—a start-up that specialized in business support software—and introduced him to the staff. Manuel endured the formalities, which he knew were nothing more than delaying tactics to give Rachel time to mount a defense against his inquiries.

"Roberto is in Seattle on a business trip," she said of her husband and business partner when they had finished the rounds. "I'm sorry you missed him."

Once they had settled in her office, Rachel said, "I suppose you're in San Francisco because of María Elena."

"Why else?" he responded sarcastically.

Rachel's demeanor remained cool, ignoring his annoyance. "I telephoned her doctor a couple of days ago, and he said she was recovering well. Is there anything new?"

"Yes, there is something new, an unusual problem. . . ."

"Problem?" She cut him off, as if she could read his mind and wanted him to stop.

Manuel studied her intently. Although Rachel was in her forties, her beauty resembled María Elena's, except that Rachel was fair-skinned, with sky-blue eyes and the younger woman was darker with sea-green eyes. He noticed the tightness of Rachel's jaw, locking her expression of calm reserve, if not one of slight arrogance.

"Well?" she said, betraying her own annoyance.

"She talks in her sleep," began Manuel.

"Really?" interrupted Rachel without a trace of irony or resentment in her voice. "So you fly out here from Mexico City to tell me that?"

"I don't mean to offend you, Rachel," said Manuel. "But all I can tell you is that she has been very restless and agitated in her sleep. She talks all night, and God only knows about what. The only word that I can understand is the name of your brother Sebastian. Perhaps if he came to see her. . . ."

"Impossible, Manuel. As I've told you before, he is not well himself."

"I don't want to seem unreasonable. I just want her to get well. Perhaps if he came and saw her, she could work out whatever it is that afflicts her mind."

Rachel resisted. "Look, Manuel, the situation is more complex than you think. What I am about to tell you makes me uncomfortable, but you leave me no alternative. The first time you asked us about Sebastian we told you he had had a nervous breakdown because we were embarrassed by the truth. But under these circumstances. . . ." She paused for a moment and collected her thoughts. "He—how can I say this?—as a young man he experimented with mind-altering drugs. We took him to a brain physiologist who believes that Sebastian is suffering some kind of mental relapse, perhaps permanent brain damage from the drugs."

"Perhaps," said Manuel skeptically. "But what if his condition is not drug induced, what if—"

"What if he's crazy and María Elena being the same blood is crazy, too? Now you sound just like my father. That's why he didn't want them to see each other. Think, Manuel, María Elena was buried alive for three days. Who wouldn't be traumatized by that experience. What she and Sebastian have is not related at all."

"What else can you tell me about him?" asked Manuel.

"Who?"

"Sebastian. What's the nature of his relationship to the rest of the family? He's not really your brother, is he?"

"He's my adopted brother, the son of Jorge Vázquez

who is my father's brother," she said.

Manuel remembered that María Elena had used those exact words when he had asked her to identify the photograph of Sebastian in her office.

"María Elena once told me that Sebastian is an artist," said Manuel already knowing of Sebastian's vocation. "He does Indian and Mexican art," María Elena had told him, "which are very popular in the United States. He also does graphic designs, you know, for book covers and artwork for video games.") Like many business people, Manuel could not fathom how a man could make a living as an artist.

"Was," responded Rachel, interrupting Manuel's mental tangent.

"Was? What do you mean?"

"Was—as in the past," said Rachel, her voice distant, as if she were speaking to herself.

"He no longer works?" inquired Manuel.

"No. He doesn't work. He doesn't do anything anymore. He is under the illusion that he is dead and that if he leaves his dwelling his flesh will decompose in the sun. He also says he is on a ship, and he goes through the motions as if he's experiencing sea sickness."

"That is. . . ." Manuel stopped himself from saying the word 'insane' for fear of offending Rachel Vázquez. He changed his tack. "When did he begin to believe these things?"

Rachel shifted ever so slightly in her chair, betraying her anxiety, and looked out of the large window that displayed the San Francisco skyline. Finally, she said, "It started after he came back from Guanajuato. He had

begun some lithographs on Colonial Mexico for a book
he was to illustrate. That was around the same time
María Elena was in Mexico with her professor as his
graduate assistant. After she finished her work with the
professor, she took some time off, supposedly to do research on the colonial period at the university in
Guanajuato. Sebastian went to join her so she could
share some of her ideas with him. They were both particularly interested in the life of Martín Cortés."

"Who?"

"As a Mexican you ought to know who Martín Cortés
is, Manuel," said Rachel. "Martín Cortés was the first
Mexican, the son of Hernán Cortés and *Doña* Marina.
Our ancestor Armando Vázquez personally knew these
people. My family has always prided itself on keeping
the memory of our ancestor's exploits alive. So it was
only natural that Sebastian would want to work on any
project related to the conquest of Mexico. In any event,
when Sebastian came back, he was unbalanced and delusional. He claimed that the spirits of Martín Cortés
and a black dog would come for him at night. He insisted, every time a dog barked, that it was Martín's
dog. My brother Ricardo had his fill one night and
dragged Sebastian out into the night to prove to him
there was no dog, no man dressed in armor as Sebastian
claimed. My mother and I pleaded with Ricardo to stop
because we could see that Sebastian was terrified of
something that night, more than other nights. There are
not many things that surprise me, Manuel, hence there
are few things that scare me, but Sebastian screams
were horrible, as if he were in some terrible pain. He

said, 'María El—' Never mind what he said. One of the neighbors even called the police. When the police questioned him, Sebastian kept saying that the spirit of Martín Cortés had robbed him of his soul. His eyes, they were no longer filled with fear, but they had lost their clarity."

"So he completely lost his mind that night," said Manuel.

"Yes, but my father refused to believe it. That is when he asked María Elena to come home and see Sebastian."

"Why her?"

"They were close, shared the same fascinations with the past and with the myths and superstitions of the Indians. My father thought perhaps she could reach him. And reach him she did. That is why my father forbid her to see him again."

"What did she do that was so terrible?"

"You insist on knowing, correct?" warned Rachel.

"Yes. I must know," said Manuel.

"María Elena told Sebastian some fantastic tale— that he had died. I think she called it the 'sleep of death,' or something like that. Ever since then, he has claimed that he is dead. She made him worse than he was. My father could not forgive her. He felt she had betrayed him."

"I am sorry. I didn't know. María Elena never told me." Manuel acted as if he were appeased but, in truth, he did not believe Rachel Vázquez had told him the entire story. He sensed that the relationship between María Elena and her parents was deeply flawed, that some emotional deformity had traumatized her to the point where some shocking event could cause her to forget her languages. But he decided not to press, knowing that Rachel would not tell him any more.

Before he left her office, Rachel Vázquez told him to, "Please be patient. We have had a difficult time these last few years. First my grandfather died, then Sebastian got ill, followed by my father's unexpected death. And now this accident. I hope you understand."

Manuel promised to be patient and returned to Mexico City that afternoon.

10

Teotihuacán

A week after Manuel returned to work, María Elena's colleagues came to visit her. It was her birthday and, thus, presented them with an opportunity to loosen Manuel's grip on her.

"We have a surprise for you," they told her as they took her with them to the car. "Don't worry about your jealous boyfriend," they assured her. "We already told him we were coming for you."

María Elena's friends had expected Manuel Muñoz to resist their idea of taking her away for the day. But he had acquiesced with a resignation that bordered on indifference. It seemed his perceptions and sensibilities had become unnaturally altered, as if María Elena's melancholy was quicksand, pulling him in with her.

For his part, he wanted desperately to recover his former rhythms, to again be absorbed by the demands of his business, the desires of materialism, the approval of his social circle. During María Elena's convalescence, his ambitious disposition had been consumed by her infirmity, his sensations diverted from the stimuli of the external world to that of the night and the fantasy of dreams. He tried to will away this malaise, and the recurring dreams of the sorcerers who persecuted him. But it was as if María Elena had come to dominate him with her malady.

After he had consented to let María Elena go, he felt guilty, as if he were passing her to another man. But he knew that his feelings were baseless, for if any of María Elena's male colleagues harbored any romantic feeling toward her, they kept those feelings well repressed. Manuel had mastered the art of telegraphing aggressive and intimidating messages that were unmistakable to any potential competitor. There was a strange aura about him, like that of a bar room brawler, despite his sophisticated and refined exterior. Perhaps it was because of the largeness of the muscles in his hands, or perhaps it was his eyes, as María Elena once told him, and how they blackened when he became angry.

María Elena's friends' birthday surprise was a visit to the ruins of Teotihuacán. They first stopped at a small cafe in a town called San Juan de Teotihuacán where they gave her a party. Afterwards they took her to an excavation site, supposedly to show her some new discoveries. When they reached the site, there was not much work done. She gave them a puzzled look.

"We're recruiting you back into our ranks," they told her. "What do you say?"

She laughed ironically, but nonetheless enthusiastically joined her colleagues.

Under the supervision of her friends her incommunicable language was no obstacle to her usefulness. She almost instantaneously recovered her skills, which she had first learned as a student. For the remainder of the day, she worked along side her friends, making notes in iconographic inscription. She recorded some of her observations in rough engineering designs, which, much to her relief, her colleagues were able to understand.

At the end of the day, María Elena separated herself from the group and ascended the mountainous Pyramid of the Sun. Her colleagues let her be, hoping that perhaps her love for solitude and the past would unlock the enigma of her strange language.

When María Elena reached the summit, she found La Nahua waiting for her.

"The city of the Gods is honored by your return, Malintzín." La Nahua spoke to María Elena in the old Mexican language. María Elena acknowledged the old woman's homage by a slight bow of the head.

La Nahua admired the young woman. "Ah, you are exactly the way the prophecies described you, except for your eyes. They are the eyes of a *mestizo*, like Martín Cortés."

"Come," said La Nahua. "Sit next to me. Let us listen for the voice in the winds."

Soon the breeze swept through the valley, bringing the whispers of a tale.

". . . *la tierra de iras y no volveras* is the world where all of your desires can be fulfilled. The eagle, who was once a man, comes to you and offers you passage to that strange and wondrous land, but you must take enough meat to feed the eagle during the journey, otherwise he will turn

on you and devour you. So either way, you never
return. You die during the passage, or you reach
iras y no volveras and never return."

"The rituals of passage to the other world is buried
with the tongues of the dead," said La Nahua. "Martín
Cortés will officiate the ceremonial breaking of the
bones after the Vernal Equinox. You must be prepared
to translate by then, Malintzín."

María Elena spoke in her Asiatic language. "? . . ."

"I do not understand you, daughter," said La Nahua.

María Elena persisted. "? . . . ? . . . ? . . ."

"So many question, daughter, and you must be the
one who finds the answers. So many enigmas, prophecies swollen in the womb of time. When our people were
conquered, the wise men said that the Eagle,
Cuauhtémoc, would return one day and liberates us
from the oppressors. But first the Gods demanded the
sacrifice of a *mestizo* son. We have waited for centuries,
the poor souls of the slaughtered Indians, almost half a
millennium of drifting and prowling in the crevices of
buildings and abandoned caves."

"? . . ." María Elena, frustrated by her own incompre-
hensibility, began to weep and asked urgently, "? . . ."

La Nahua pointed to the south and said, "Uxmal."

11

Iberia, 1528-87

Many centuries ago, in the town of Villarreal in Extremadura, a sailor named Armando Vázquez arrived and settled and never once returned to his native land of Castile. He was one of the small group of men who had participated in the destruction of the Aztec world. He told stories of a great city of gold, and feathered warriors. In his possession was a land grant from the King of Spain himself. Unlike many of the men of the Conquest, he declined to build himself a fiefdom in the New World, certain that the malevolent spirit who had given them the power to destroy the Indian world would someday demand retribution. However, in his old age, he took what money he had acquired from the spoils of the Conquest and, from the safety of his home in Extremadura, ordered that a house be built in the New World. When it was finished, he had it furnished and locked.

"It is a house for the spirit of Martín Cortés," said the reluctant conquistador, after the disappearance of Martín the Elder, the hero of the battle of Argel. "May he someday find peace in death."

Armando Vázquez constantly thought of the fall of
Tenochtitlán and felt sorry for its destroyed beauty. He
retold the story of the death of the great city to whoever
would lend his ear, as if with each recounting the
memory would expel itself from his spirit. He spoke of
broken idols, streets and canals awash in blood; the
roaring of flames that drowned the cries of children, old
men and desperate women. Like many of the Spaniards
of the Conquest, he had been infatuated by the beauty
and extraordinary intelligence of Malintzín, the
commander's woman. He had loved and pitied the half-
breed son of Cortés, wished the boy had been his, had
been amazed at the beauty of his green eyes, and had
seen in a dream the boy's eyes devoured by insects.

He never returned to Mexico because of that dream,
seeing it as a bad omen. "I prefer to remember Martín
the way he was, with his beautiful eyes," he said.

Moreover, solely on premonition, Armando Vázquez
made a strange request to his old friend, Bernal Díaz del
Castillo while the latter was composing his memoirs on
the conquest of Mexico. In a letter dictated to his son,
Armando Vázquez asked that his name not be included
in the chronicles of the Conquest. The son, never forget-
ting the letter, passed on its contents to later generations. The letter said:

> Let me die in oblivion, old friend. Perhaps my
> descendants can escape the curse we have brought
> upon ourselves for the sins of destruction.

The Mariner, Armando Vázquez

Bernal Díaz del Castillo did as his friend had asked,

and the name Vázquez disappeared from the annals of the Conquest. Armando Vázquez also forbade his sons to go to Mexico.

"Let the land heal itself, mother that she is," he told them. "Do not even remember me and my misguided deeds because the spirits will read your minds and find you and the hidden sins I have condemned you with."

So a great-nephew of the old man, posing as a grandson, went to Mexico in 1583, and through legal maneuvering, claimed the same lands in the name of the Mariner Armando Vázquez. José María Vázquez moved into a mansion he built in Mérida and became an important farmer. Not surprisingly, the reputation of the old conquistador conveyed to the nephew the status of royalty. However, by the time the revolution of 1910 had arrived, the old mansion lay in disrepair, as if time had avenged itself against great arrogance of the *Criollos*. The descendants of the nephew, now Mexicans and not Castilians, locked up the great house and left for the United States, where no one would compare their current poverty to their former splendor.

As for the conquistador, Armando Vázquez, the old man died in self-imposed solitude and his children, infected by the silent currents of his memory, dreamt of crumbling stone and old wooden ships and men who turned themselves into birds. Generations passed, but the dreams remained, as if the people were merely inhabiting the dreams. Sometimes at night, they would see a black dog run across the yard and hear the whistles of a man, a sad, barely heard tune, a song tossed to oblivion. In the morning they would say, "The spirit of Martín came again to look for *el viejito* Armando, but he's in hell because he went with Cortés when they destroyed the city."

The Vázquez family, despite their ancestor's admonition, preserved their legacy of the New World. Their most treasured heirloom was a copy of the land grant given to Armando Vázquez by the king of Spain. And many times, they, the descendants of Armando Vázquez, would take out the old land deed and touch and smell the parchment, for it was soiled with dirt from another land. And they knew that the answer to their enigmatic dreams was buried in this land. It was their greatest desire to cross the ocean as their ancestor had, to find the land that smelled like the parchment.

12

Uxmal

María Elena found a way to communicate what she wanted: with her drawings. When Manuel Muñoz came home on her birthday, he found the kitchen table littered with María Elena's sketches of pyramids and other schematics of an inscrutable nature. When she saw him, she brought him a map and pointed to the ruins of Uxmal.

"No!" he said emphatically, not wanting her to return to the place of her unfortunate accident. But she was persistent, refusing to go anywhere with him to celebrate her birthday. She responded to his pleas for her cooperation by again showing him the map and pointing to the ancient city, as if to say, "take me there."

The following week, Manuel reluctantly drove her to the Yucatán. He had made arrangements to stay in Mérida with his cousin Pablo Muñoz, his best friend since childhood. Pablo was single and, thus, Manuel thought he could avoid the intrusions and potential gossip of in-laws.

When they arrived in Uxmal, María Elena immediately went to the Pyramid of the Magician, as if she were looking for something she had lost. Manuel stayed behind and watched her from a distance as she then moved away from the pyramid and walked towards that part of the ancient city that was still unrestored. He followed her at a discreet distance so as to not disturb her, but close enough to keep her within his reach. Suddenly, María Elena stopped at a doorway into one of the ruins, and appeared to melt into the air, as if she were an illusion. Manuel Muñoz blinked and squinted his eyes. He could swear that María Elena had become transparent, as if she were dissolving into another reality.

"She is looking for her lover," a voice said from behind him.

He swung around and saw an old Indian woman. "What did you say?" he said irritably.

"*La muchacha*, there," said La Nahua, pointing to María Elena. "She is looking for her lover. I will speak with her."

Manuel grabbed the old woman, furious at her intrusion and her implication. "I am her fiancé."

"But you are alive, *Señor*," said La Nahua, astonished.

"What are you saying, *vieja loca?*"

"See for yourself, see how she enters the portal. She has lost her way. Perhaps the soldier's dog will help her find her way back. . . ."

Manuel Muñoz pushed the old woman away and rushed to retrieve his fiancée. Frightened by the strangeness of the old woman, Manuel Muñoz immediately drove himself and María Elena to Mérida, to return to what he considered the safety of a living city.

The combination of what he had just witnessed, the ancient Indian city itself, and the old woman's ramblings had somehow evoked a buried memory in Manuel, the sensation of a primitive fear, one of abandonment and debasement that he had experienced as a child.

His father, a civil engineer with the government, had once taken Manuel with him to visit a water drainage project in one of the slums. Manuel remembered that while his father inspected the project, he had cowered inside the car, watching the people of the local neighborhood as if they were beasts, nearly suffocated by the smell of rotting sewage, human sweat, and grease laden foods. That memory, for some reason, he associated with his recurring nightmare of being swallowed by the earth during an earthquake, a dream he had tried to force himself to forget, calling it nonsense, childish superstitions. But his pretense of skepticism merely intensified his secret fear that his dream was a premonition.

Thus, he never spoke of it to anyone. Nor did it ever occur to him to mention it to María Elena who—he did not know—would have understood it.

While they drove back to Mérida, the sleepy sound of motion upon the road and the cyclical rhythm of the engine brought back his nightmare in fullest detail. Manuel recalled the gray, claustrophobic skies, the low trees, the sensation of pursuit, the diabolical and frenzied eyes of the sorcerers, and the sweating green and white paint on their faces. By the time he and María Elena arrived at his cousin's house, Manuel wore the look of a man who had had an encounter with death.

"What's wrong, Manuel?" asked his cousin Pablo.

Manuel said nothing of his inner fears. Instead he told his cousin of María Elena, "I am worried that she will never get well."

Later that night when Manuel went outside to the patio to forget his insomnia, he found a letter crumpled on the ground. The note said:

Querida,

> If you will only say one word, the one that will free me, I will come for you again. Let their laws be damned.

> S.

Perplexed by the cryptic message, Manuel took the letter and went back up to the room his cousin had graciously provided for him and his fiancée. María Elena was asleep and in the middle of a fit of dreams filled with songs, parts of which she sang throughout the night. In the morning she was able to speak a few words of Spanish for the first time since her accident.

"I want to confess, Manuel. Take me to a church."

"Are you well again?" he asked urgently, for although she was again comprehensible, his mouth could taste the bitter, nervous bile that was forming in his stomach.

"I only have so many words. Please take me to a church!"

He took her to a church in Mérida. He didn't know what it was called, nor would he remember later. Once inside the church, she immediately sought confession. Moments later, a priest emerged from the confessional bewildered. Manuel quickly went to the confessional to get María Elena who was still narrating her repentance, but not in Spanish anymore. She was again speaking in the melancholic tones of her Asiatic language.

13

Refractions of Memory

The faces in the old photograph stared back with
the patience of corpses, gestures fatalistically
frozen in a contraction of time. Some of the faces
were more pensive than others. Still, others gazed into
the photographer's instrument with half-hopeful smiles,
as if to brave the formless fogs of their destinies. The
youngest of the children sat on their parents' laps,
their smallish images faded, as if they were apparitions
of desire and not real humans. The men, even the most
melancholic ones, all looked more self-assured than the
women, as if their masculinity would one day protect
them from the sadness and longing that precedes death.

'It must be because women bring life into the world,'
said Father Fernando Ocampo to himself as he observed
the old group photograph of his relatives at his grand-
parents' fiftieth wedding anniversary. Since his recent
encounter with the night voice of Sebastian the Mariner,
Fernando Ocampo had taken to looking at the old photographs that he had brought with him from Querétaro.

He surveyed the photograph again, finding his own
face as a child, seated on the floor in the front row. The

child, Fernando, looks off to the left, away from the camera, his expression dreamy and unconcerned with the moment at hand.

Fernando Ocampo's memory of that day was like the photograph, in black and white, as if he were remembering an old movie. He again looked at each face and called it by its name.

'This one is my uncle Gregorio, the grain dealer, who had one scale for buying and another for selling . . . this one is my aunt Govita whose husband was a homosexual and the people said that her children were really fathered by another man . . . this one is my cousin Raimundo, the army lieutenant executed in the Revolution. . . .'

And a voice in the wind intruded with its own memories.

> "*Querida*, do you remember what *Abuelito* Gustavo used to say?"

Fernando Ocampo knew that it was him, Sebastian. The old priest listened in his alcoholic-like trance of wakefulness, eavesdropping on the wind that carried its own remembrance. . . .

> "Remember how he used to talk about the old house in Mérida, how it lay abandoned for over eighty years after the revolution? And before that, how the old Mariner Vázquez forbade his offspring to go to the New World? For generations we knew that the wrong Vázquez—the old Mariner's nephew—had taken possession of the lands in Mexico. But in the delayed cycles of justice, the

lands of old Vázquez were repossessed by the Indians after the revolution. It was bound to happen because our ancestor had warned them not to possess stolen lands, and *Abuelito* Gustavo, ever the republican, used to say, 'Good for Zapata and *los indios*. The land belonged to them first. Who was the king of Spain to give it to a bunch of bastards anyway?' That's the way *Abuelito* used to think, always on the Indians' side even though he was a Spaniard. That was his dream, to go to the New World, not to possess it, but to become possessed by it, devoured by its lurid dreams. With Franco and his gang running the country, they thought it best to leave, to find another life, especially after the authorities had accused my father of murdering a policeman. But *Abuelito* Gustavo would have found a way to come to Mexico, even if *Papá* José and my real father had wanted to stay in Spain. *Abuelito* Gustavo wanted to fulfill his old man's desire to die in the New World. 'I want to smell the earth of my dreams,' he would say. You know the stories, do you not, *amor*? I never cared so much for the stories as I did for the old man's dreams, the way he'd talk about the old mansion that José María Vázquez had built in Mérida as if he had been there. What was the name of *el viejito marinero* Vázquez? His Christian name? I cannot remember it right now because the ocean will not still itself. Can you ask him in your dream tonight?

"María Elena, how I remembered you last night, especially your *quinceañera*. That was the last time I remember you happy, but no, you say you were happy later, when we went to the old house to look for the spirit of Martín Cortés. I remember telling you, 'We will have to see a bruja.' And you were not afraid at all, and you even saw Martín's dog. The bruja said we were destined to find the spirit of Martín Cortés and the world stopped spinning, and it was the same day for the longest time. And I said to you, 'I wonder how the people on the other side can live in darkness.' And you said, 'They are still dreaming that it is the same night.'

"But that is not what I remembered about you last night. It was your *quinceañera*, and how you grew up so suddenly. Ricardo said I had to be at your party regardless of how I felt about *Papá* José, and I did want you to know that I had missed you, but I figured when you grew up you'd find me again. You wouldn't have to ask permission. . . . Ricardo said, 'He believes any lie over the truth, Sebastian. I know *Tía* was an honorable woman and a virgin when your father married her. That talk about her being the priest's mistress is a ridiculous lie. Old men are cuckolded in their imaginations.'

"But she was still my mother, and *Papá* José said those things about her after she was dead and couldn't defend herself. You understand, you of all people understand. You have understood since you were little that you were destined for sin, just like me. I went inside my mother's picture once, and she said, 'You will pay for the injustices done to Martín Cortés, *hijo*.'"

14

Manuel

As they drove back to Mexico City the day after María Elena had momentarily regained her language and confessed at the church in Mérida, it occurred to Manuel that even before her accident she had not spoken a great deal. At first he found it charming and a challenge to conquer. But now the memory of her few words was even more haunting, how she had told him when she became his lover, "I am not your conquest, Manuel. I am going with you because I choose to, not because I am deceived by words."

And that was all she said, but by then it was too late because in his efforts to seduce her, he had fallen in love with her. So much so that he broke off his companionship with one of his best friends when the latter jokingly said of her, "I'll take her when you are finished with her, Manuel."

He remembered the times before her accident, when they would spend the night together. How, even in her sleep, she seemed detached, as if she were living another life, and would many times wake up more tired than when she went to bed. When he asked her once why she was always so quiet, she said, "Because I talk in my dreams all night." Many times, when they spent hours walking arm in arm in Chapultepec Park, she would silently watch the surroundings, as if in a waking dream, as if she were simultaneously experiencing the events of another reality. At first, unconcerned with her internal mind wanderings and engrossed with his own thoughts about his work, he welcomed her silence, considered it refreshing compared to the pouting jealousies of his former girlfriends. He mistook her silence for respect, thinking that she was deferring to his importance as her boyfriend. However, progressively, her silence began to irritate him, leading him to believe that she was rebelling against his presence.

Once, during a Sunday walk in the park, he said to her, "Did you hear what I just said?" although he had said nothing, lying so as to deceive her into revealing her mind.

Without malice, she responded, "No, I wasn't listening to you."

Several times, when he touched her in the middle of her sleep, she responded with the logic of a dreamer: "There are ships in the middle of the desert," or "She is weeping by the causeway."

They had become engaged to be married under unusual circumstances. His family, at first, was opposed to the very idea of a marriage. They thought, of course, that like most Mexican women from the United States, she had no true sense of her place in the family. 'God knows women act like men in that country. They think nothing of taking lovers without any remorse.'

Like everyone else, they were unconsciously suspicious of her extreme beauty, which was like a deforming disease in that it diverted attention away from the elements of her heart, her true identity.

María Elena was well aware of this predicament, that beauty like ugliness allows the observer to indulge in his or her worst fears and most perverse fantasies. Like her sister, Rachel, she had set out early in life to construct an unassailable defense against the effects of her beauty by accumulating college degrees, and by overindulging in work. Still, despite her accomplishments and integrity, Manuel's family only visualized her as a bad woman.

Manuel, who at this juncture of their relationship was completely in love with her, was angry that he couldn't defend her honor because his family knew she was his lover, but did not object to their affair as long as he did not marry her. Also, he knew that their instincts about her having another lover before him were true. He had asked her once, in what he now remembered as a rare moment of complete trust between them.

They had just returned to Mexico City from Cuernavaca, after having spent the weekend together. He had made her happy that weekend, letting her draw him into her fascination with the past. "You be my tour guide," he told her when they went to visit Hernán Cortés's palace. She opened up to him as never before. He had always known that she was highly intelligent, but he was surprised at the sophistication of her knowledge. She recounted the events of the past with the flair of a story teller, as if she had been an eye witness.

As soon as they left Cuernavaca, María Elena's rare talkative enthusiasm faded back to her dreamy introspections and continued for the rest of the day. In the evening, they were sitting together on the terrace of Manuel's house when he asked her, "Have you been with any man besides me?"

"Yes," she said, without hesitation, shame or self-defensiveness. "Only with one man."

"And?" asked Manuel, taken aback by her frankness.

"We could not marry, so he left me," she responded and retreated into her silence.

This knowledge, like a hidden virus that rouses itself to life, awoke in him an intense longing to possess her thoughts and thus her being. But she withheld the mystery of herself from him although she was faithful to him and loyal to his dreams and aspirations.

After she had made this revelation to him, whenever her eyes opened from sleep, he knew it was not his face that was reflected in her eyes, nor was the scent on her skin his after he'd make love to her. She would awaken as if from the embrace of her first lover, whose essence had become a part of her, as natural as breathing. This other lover had penetrated the shadows of her defenseless night, and she carried him from within as one carries imagination, perpetually reappearing in one's waking consciousness and in the remote wells of sleep.

Part of Manuel wanted to lash out, but he knew that he had no real rival. She had said so herself that she and her first lover could not marry, but Manuel was annoyed that in her asylum of silence she constantly re-created her first lover's being. Manuel's senseless jealousy caused him to leave her once.

"I can't live with a mute!" he told her.

"And if I talked, Manuel, you would complain about the sound of my voice," she responded. "You are just like all men. Perhaps we are better off without each other."

Her non-resistance infuriated him because he knew that although she could live with him, she did not need him. If he left her, she would forget about him because she was not in love with him. He could not define her by the common conventions. With the exception of her first lover and himself, she had had no romantic involvement with other men. She seemed, in her own manner, to conform to the standards of propriety. And despite her professional achievements, she lacked what he perceived as the aggressive nature of other modern women. She was, for the most part, utterly reserved and serious. She seemed completely at ease only in the company of her archeologist friends.

With them, she revealed her sense of humor and a lighter nature. Only at their request would she sing, which was one of her talents Manuel had not known about. After she lost her language, Manuel recalled that even before he had heard her sing, her voice resonated with a musical quality, as if she possessed a different language of pure sound that was devoid of syntax. He began to suspect that if he stayed away from her for a short period of time, she would lose her desire for him. If her imagination had been merely occupied by another man, he could have found a way to reclaim her. But there was something much more complicated about her solitude.

Once he came by her office unexpectedly to surprise her. She was working quietly, reconstructing some artifacts. There was a sad aura about her, like that of the deformed, old beggars who sat outside of the churches, a dreamer's aspiration of the heavens. She seemed more than just consumed by her passion for her work, as if the artifacts were agents from the past that devoured her spirit as the price for her knowledge.

Whenever he asked her about the nature of her research, the answers she gave implied that she seemed not to be searching for conventional interpretations of history, but for a remote secret, a special knowledge that would connect her to the past. He wanted not only to rescue her from that 'thing,' but to destroy it. 'What else does she want that I can't give her? What other life can be better than the one we've both achieved?' The possibility that she wanted to be free from his world secretly haunted his few dreams.

After they quarreled, he left her for a month and when he sought her out again, she had gone home to San José, California, to visit her family. Desperately wanting her back, he forced himself to go to California and beg her to forgive him. To spare himself further humiliation in front of her family, he introduced himself as her fiancé, even though he had not yet asked her to marry him.

"Is this true, María Elena," asked José Vázquez, her father. "Is this man your fiancé?"

Her response was, "He says he is, so he must be."

The Vázquez family, and later the Muñoz family, accepted their alleged engagement with grudging resignation. Neither thought it was a good match. The Vázquez clan found Manuel to be conceited and elitist; Manuel's family questioned María Elena's morals. Only later when Manuel's family found out that her people were directly and legitimately descended from the conquistadors would they openly embrace her. It was their opportunity to authenticate their arrogance. Although the Muñoz family had recently risen from the ranks of the working classes, they now had acquired upper-class aspirations and pretensions for their offspring, divorcing themselves from their humble roots and their Indian identity, seeing it as inferior to the European. They spoke disparagingly of *los indios* and *los pobres*, the Indians and the poor. They tried to enlist María Elena, whose European blood they found ennobling, to vindicate their self-aggrandizement, as if to say, "You are better than this garbage who are littered throughout our city and you ought to recognize one of your own."

But, as usual, she was non compliant, refusing to give in to illusions. She strongly adhered to her family's Spanish political liberalism and considered the Muñoz's class consciousness as parochial and mean-spirited.

"I'm nothing special. I'm an ordinary Mexican just like the rest of you," she said once during a society party at Manuel's parents' house.

"But your father is a descendant of important people," protested *Doña* Teofila, Manuel's mother.

That remark incensed María Elena, but she remained silent just long enough to find the words to tactfully rebut Manuel's mother in front of her society friends.

"My father's people have been simple, honest workers. He married a Mexican woman whose people were simple workers as well," she said finally. "I am like the rest of you."

Manuel was appalled, but conquered by her frankness. Yet he had found his mother's comments embarrassing, making his family look insecure and uncouth in front of his fiancé.

"Why can't we just be Mexicans," he countered, taking María Elena's side, trying to save face.

María Elena gave him a surprisingly gentle look of approval.

Later that evening, she smiled and simply said, "I'll fall in love with you, I think." He thought she was joking.

15

The Land With Three Moons

It was after Fernando Ocampo had spent the Holy Week in Dolores Hidalgo that he decided to write down his night visions and the conversations in the winds. He had, for some time, felt the urgent need to confide in someone and share his solitary nocturnal visions, as if by doing so he could make them real and encounter those dream actors in his waking reality. Fernando Ocampo had gone to Dolores Hidalgo for that very purpose. Disguised as a layman, he intended to confess his night visions to another priest. But once inside the confessional, he changed his mind and made up a phony sin, for which the confessor promptly forgave him.

During the bus trip back to Mexico City, he resolved to write a journal for Lupe Huerta, the daughter of his deceased niece Alicia Ocampo. 'She was not even fifty,' thought Fernando bitterly of his favorite niece Alicia, the only relative to whom he'd been able to completely open his heart, perhaps because her suffering had made her wise beyond her years.

Alicia Ocampo, his younger brother Juan's daughter, had been lured to the great city like many young people in the 1960's. She came to look for work and the excitement lacking in small, provincial towns like Querétaro. Father Fernando helped procure her work as a maid in a household of two elderly and devout Christian women, carefully steering his niece away from employment where she could be exposed to the sexual advances of a wealthy householder or his sons. But his young niece soon fell into the trap of Ramiro Huerta, the young and rising boxer from the slums of Mexico City. 'That one had a way with women,' thought Father Fernando, recalling the athletic, masculine beauty of Ramiro Huerta. Father Fernando and Ramiro's mother—a pious Christian woman—pressured Ramiro Huerta into marrying Alicia after he had impregnated her. That was the one action in his life that Father Fernando regretted, for Ramiro Huerta went on to devastate his niece's life, leading, he was certain, to her premature death the previous year. 'How Alicia suffered!' thought Fernando, recalling the constant humiliations his niece endured: the mistresses that her husband made no effort to hide, the drinking and, at times, the beatings.

After Alicia died, Fernando, perhaps out of habit, continued to visit his niece's house in San Juan de Teotihuacán, a small town outside of Mexico City. The only member of the family to receive him with genuine warmth was Alicia's daughter, Lupe. Neither Ramiro nor his sons paid much attention to the silent grieving of the old priest.

This remembrance weighed down his heart. Hypnotized by the hum of the engine and the humidity of the breath and sweat emitted by the crowded bodies inside the bus, Fernando alternated between dozing naps and fits of wakefulness. Through half-opened eyes, he saw the world of his nocturnal visions materialize.

"Come. I am dreaming of Sebastian and his grandfather Pedro, " he heard a woman's voice say inside the dream. "They are lost in a desert of lunar rocks, a land with three moons."

Fernando, startled at the sound of the voice, woke with a tremor. That was the first time he had heard that voice, but in his heart he knew it was she, the one Sebastian had called María Elena. Like a drowning man, he again sunk into the wavy depths of his dream. In his vision he saw. . . .

A storm, a powerful force of pestilence was following Sebastian and the grandfather. The old man said to Sebastian, "Rising Eagle, fly ahead of the storm, and see if the animals have outrun it."

"Take one of my languages, Cuauhtlehuanitl," said María Elena through the winds. Sebastian spread himself before the wind and chanted a song in a forgotten tongue that María Elena had given him.

The wind transformed him into an eagle, and he flew away. When he returned, he changed the old man into a coyote so that he, too, like the other animals, could outrun the storm.

A child screamed, and Fernando felt an object hit his face. The child, his eyes filled with the remote malice of an ancestral beast, had thrown an empty paper cup straight at Fernando's head. The child's mother quickly apprehended him and apologized to the priest. The child malevolently stared at Fernando as his mother dragged him back to his seat. Not wanting to lose his dream-vision, Fernando closed his eyes again and the vision materialized once again.

Fernando and a young woman were inside a large room of an ancient stone house, older than the times of the Conquest. Fernando could clearly see her and recognized her. It was she, the woman who had visited him in his first vision of Sebastian.

"Is it you? Sebastian's María Elena?"

"Come this way," she said, appearing not to have heard him.

They kept going deeper into a stone complex. He could hear people weeping on the other side of the wall. Funeral dirges were spoken in a forgotten language accompanied by the sad songs of flutes.

Time passed. A soldier, dressed in the armour of centuries passed, sat in the shadows. The solider took them to a man-made cave where Sebastian was imprisoned. Sebastian and Fernando began digging and removing bones. They cleaned the bones and placed them in the window-like caverns on the walls. When they had finished, Sebastian and Fernando took the bones to a secret pit. There the bones were broken and ground. As the bones were splintered, voices were released. María Elena listened to the voices and translated for the soldier.

"The friars cut your mother's tongue before they

buried her, *Don* Martín."

Once Fernando had returned home and unpacked his bags, still disguised as a layman, he went to the Plaza of Santo Domingo. He walked for a while and bought a journal at a small book and magazine stand. He sat on a bench and composed the first of many journal entries. He wrote:

April 2

Estimada Lupita,

Hija, when I was a boy, I heard it spoken that those who cannot sleep begin to dream the dreams of others as if they were their own. To dream another's dream, to hear the whispers tossed about by these Mexican winds that circle back and forth through this morass of time—that is the gift of the non-sleepers. They said—the old ones—that the wind is the messenger of lovers, but that the insomniacs are the thieves of dreams.

In this journal I shall record the narratives of the winds and dreams. Perhaps you will think me insane, but this is all that I, an old and broken man, can offer you, my dearest niece.

Fernando Ocampo

Nearly a month would pass before Fernando made another journal entry. He wrote:

May 1st

Mi querida Lupita,

Tonight I am spinning in the many dreams of the sleepers, but they will not remember them. I and the other sleepless ones are keeping their dreams. How sweet are the many images given me by my insomnia. I had heard it said, many years ago in my town, that at night the soul leaves the body and journeys to other places. It is thus that I am the witness to the narratives of the night. The many deaths, the violations, the subjugation of man's bright angel are remembered in the caves of night. Only the distant lights of forgotten stars guide the dreamers back into the inertia of the waking.

But do not think that only the vulgarity is remembered. There—although you may be skeptical, not that I blame you, *hija*—in the many memories are the rumors of true life, not the mere biological procession towards death and the rebirth of the elements, but another existence, the realization of the forgotten nexus, remembered only in the sordid imaginations of outcasts. Soon, when the sun reaches it zenith, yes, more than in other times, there will be the transformation of eagles and men. Do not ask me to explain this within the conventions of the reasoning of men, Lupita. I can only grasp the true meaning of this rumor in the intoxication of the many dreams, the voices absorbed by the molecules of air.

The wind carries a whisper, his, Sebastian Vázquez, the one called the Mariner by his phantom captors. I will write down his words as I hear them. He is saying:

"Tell me a secret, *amor*. They say the Trickster of

Forgetfulness will demand that you give him your memories during the passage. But if another who passes with you possesses one of your secrets, then memory will be returned to you by a woman called *La Doña del Olvido*. Now, tell me, *amor*, send me your thoughts with the winds born of volcanoes. . . ."

Hija, his voice has disappeared. Now I see a light burning through my ceiling, but it is not fire. It is a light shinning through frozen dreams of the centuries. I see an ancient seaport, yes, with large wooden ships. The city is covered by the sun's resplendent whiteness, a jewel of light and blues. I see the hidden chambers of an alchemist. Two men are making a pact. . . .

16

Seaport of Cádiz, Spain, 1587

T he young, dark, Moorish Sorcerer looked into the scarred, once-handsome face of the green-eyed man, eyes and skin confused by the contradictions of blood. "What is your request, *Don* Martín?"

"You are Abdullah ibn Humega, said to be the most powerful *morisco* sorcerer in Spain, are you not, brother?"

The young Moorish sorcerer smiled speaking with his eyes, "yes." Any man who came to see him could be a spy of the Inquisition. Like many of his people—the Iberian Moors—he had falsely converted to Christianity to save himself. But even among his people, Abdullah ibn Humega was an outcast, for it was rumored that he practiced the black arts of pagan sorcerers. He had learned to protect his identity through stealth, allowing the nature of a given conversation to bear out the truth of his visitor's intentions.

"Speak your mind, *Don* Martín."

"I, too, have the blood of wizards in my veins," said Martín Cortés. "But I lack the knowledge to break from the prisons of time. You have the power of the ancients.

Return me to my youth, Brother Abdullah."

"And for what purpose?"

"I vowed to avenge myself," said Martín.

"Perhaps you have confused revenge with justice. I cannot be your teacher, *Don* Martín. You shall be avenged, but death shall be your teacher. You shall find solutions for your people in the anxious night of death. We, my brother sorcerers and I, shall burn your remains and you will be transformed into an eternal earth-walker until you are fulfilled."

"Brother Abdullah, death is a lonely place. Let me have a companion lest my solitude diminish my anger and my purpose," said Martín.

"You cannot take another," said the sorcerer.

"At least let me have my dog," pleaded Martín.

The young sorcerer proceeded to slaughter the black dog along with his master and burned their remains together. From the smoke emerged the youthful form of the soldier, Martín Cortés, and his black dog, the two vibrant earth-walkers, untouched by the cycles of seasons.

Thinking he had fooled the sorcerer, Martín set out on a journey to destroy his own birth as well as the lives of his inquisitors. But the young sorcerer had divined his true purpose and closed the portal to the past. Martín was condemned to travel forward in time, so that he could meet another greater destiny, completing the cycles foretold by his mother's people, and, perhaps, learning to love without the temptations of a man.

Martín's spirit, which had retained the memories and bitterness of himself as an old man, raced through the strata of time, until he found a multilingual woman with a *mestizo* child in her womb. When he found the woman, he called her Malintzín, cut the child from her womb, and spread the child's blood on the altars of the gods of his mother's people. As the gods devoured its blood, the smoke of his hatred lifted from his death dream, bringing the clarity of sorrow.

The Moorish sorcerer's spirit, who had witnessed Martín's hateful act from the corridors of the past, stepped forth from the carved stones of the abandoned Aztec temple.

"*Don* Martín, what do you now see?"

"I see myself being dreamed," answered Martín.

"Follow the sights of the dreamers, *Don* Martín."

"What is it that I must find?"

"Remember the prophecy given to your mother on the night of her first menstrual blood. Gather the voices silenced by death before the sun's zenith. . . ." The sorcerer's shade and voice faded from the vision of Martín Cortés. His soldier's spirit set out to capture the wandering ghosts of the slaughtered Cholulan priests as he embarked on his final campaign.

17

Father Fernando's Journal

May 10th

Mi querida Lupita,

Today, a letter arrived, without a return address, the envelope crumpled, the post mark indistinguishable and a blanched spot where the stamp had been. It is written in the language of dreams, but I can understand it. As I read the letter, my ears become filled with the voice of a woman who haunts my dreams. Sebastian calls her María Elena. She is the one who wrote it. I will translate the letter for you, Lupita. It says. . . .

Mi querido Sebastian,

So I must let you know at last that I kept a secret from you. I never meant to, but after Pedro Eloy Joaquín found us together, I wanted to keep the conception of our child a secret until after we left Montemorelos. I was afraid—and my fear was prophetic—that he would tell our adoptive parents and our life together would be destroyed. I knew that what we had done revolted

113

him. The ancient laws of his people and mine condemned the union of kin, and we were more than that, and less.

Even after *Mamá* Silvia and Rachel came for me, I was going to find you and tell you, but soon after we were separated, I was carried away in a night vision to Uxmal. There a masked high priest cut me open and killed the child. Rachel told me I was having a bad dream, that my hallucination was being created by the pain of the miscarriage. But I tell you, no, it was the other way around. I was cut open, I saw my already formed child with his pathetic look of a sea-creature, unable to marvel at the horror of his death. Even today, only I can see the crude scar across my belly. The bleeding I had was too massive and too sudden to be a miscarriage.

Rachel and *Mamá* were talking in the hospital room while I was anesthetized. I could hear them speaking as if in a dream, as I hear you all the time, suspended between the material world and my despair. *Mamá* Silvia said that the child's death was God's will, his punishment for my incest.

As I write this, Lupita, I am inside of this memory. As if the letter were a medium of time, I experience the sensation of that moment, like a phantom spying on the living. I speak through other voices, I become these others. I hear them saying. . . .

"God has punished her for her sin."

"And what of me, *Mamá*? Has God continued to punish me?"

Fernando temporarily awoke from his visions. He could feel the rushing wind again, penetrating his frail body. But he did not stop writing, fearful of losing his connection to the world of air and dreams.

Lupita, the voices from another time fade, and I lose the ability to read the rest of the letter.

Sebastian the Mariner, the one she is writing to, cannot find her letters, *hija*. Only if I translate them for him will he hear her message, for I dream and speak with her.

At that moment, Fernando heard Sebastian's voice enter his room. A voice so clear that had Fernando closed his eyes, he could swear Sebastian was not speaking from a vast distance through the winds, but there, in the same room, as if he had come for a special and private confession.

Lupita, I can hear him now. He is now speaking to her, emptying his heart. Am I the mediator between these lost lovers? I hear him saying. . . .

"Beloved, by the time you were born, *Papá* José and *Mamá* Silvia lost their desire to go to Mexico. Death had become associated with that land, not just the death of people, but of the purity of the aspirational dreams of the young. Mexico reminded them of the futility of the dream of happiness. It was as if from that land a dark cloud, a pestilence, had grown out of the collective frustrations of a people conquered in everything except their silence. They saw Ramiro Huerta that way, an avenger of a generational frustration. His violation of their daughter was as anonymous as the collective anger of the dispossessed. They even considered the moody surliness of Ricardo and the mindless merriment of Josesito as a contagion absorbed from their stay in Mexico when they were avoiding the Vietnam war.

"But, María Elena, it was not always like that. I remember after I came to live with them how every year they took us to Coahuila and Nuevo Leon to see *Mamá's* family, and *Papá* would take me and the boys to the desert to see my other grandfather, Pedro Eloy Joaquín. That was when *Mamá's* parents were still alive. They died two years before you were born, within a month of each other, and so *Mamá* was the first to suggest that they not return. 'What's the use of going now, José?' she would say. 'There's nothing left but sadness.'

"But it was your being born that made them stop. *Papá* even sold out his interest in the business in Nuevo Leon. After all of those years, *Papá* remembered his own homeland. 'We can go now that that son of bitch is dead,' said *Papá* of Franco, and that is how they substituted Spain for Mexico.

"But politics was not *Papa's* true motive. Perhaps your birth—you are your great-grandmother Elena's namesake—reminded him that he had not seen the grave of his mother in decades, and perhaps he felt remorse for having buried *Abuelito*

Gustavo so far from her. . . ."

Another rush of wind blew in through the open wind, stealing with it Sebastian's voice. Fernando waited patiently in the stillness of the night for time itself to begin to compress before his eyes like vegetation weighed down by rain. As the layers of time twisted before his eyes, he could now not only hear events of the past unfold, but actually see them recreate themselves as if in a phantasmagoric theater. He feverishly continue to record what he saw and heard.

Lupita, I can see him now. He is speaking, as if in a vertigo of love, the sensation of floating vapors entering his ears, penetrating his brain. And he can see it all as it had been for centuries, the dusty *norteño pueblos*, the ancient adobe houses, walls still riddled with bullets fired from Apache guns. The Indian memories remaining unconquered, recalling the nomadic origins of their Asiatic ancestors. Sebastian begins his narrative again . . . .

"In *Mamá's pueblo*, there were some very old people who still remembered the last Indian raids. The people would hide their daughters in Lucas Villarreal's house because his was the oldest and most fortified. I remember the old ones: *Mamá's* mother, a mixed blood woman who could have been taken for an Indian if it had not been for her green eyes; and her father, a blond man who could recite the names of his people dating back four hundred years. . . ."

The night voice momentarily paused, as if to allow Fernando a moment to ponder the fragment of time that floated in the air. As he was drawn deeper into the chasm in the fabric of time, the old man was filled with the very sensation of the lovers. He wrote:

Lupita, I have just realized that Sebastian is not speaking to her at this very moment. It is another time that has now past. It is his memory of her that I am witnessing. I see her in his arms. Sebastian stops to listen for her breathing, so primal in its fluid indifference, mere life, a mystery of oceans and windstorms. And unchanged from her first breath, pregnant with unformed words.

He tells her. . . .

"It was destiny, *querida*, that *Mamá* was sent to secretarial school in Monterrey and met *Papá*. Because just outside of Montemorelos, where her uncles and cousins still live, was the house called '*la casa del bulto*.' People have called it that for hundreds of years and wondered who had built a two-story, hacienda style house in the middle of nowhere and left it locked. From the cracks in the doors and windows, one could even see the furniture—a modest version of sixteenth century wealth. The house invited the curiosity of generations of children. *Mamá* Silvia and some of her cousins actually got inside. Can you imagine the coincidence that she would someday marry the descendant of the builder of the house. . . . María Elena, *amor*, are you listening to me?"

Sebastian feels her dreamer's movement in the dark.

"Yes" she says, her voice thickened with the night. "I am dreaming your words."

Her hand moves from his shoulder to the depression in his neck, caresses his skin.

"Tell me the rest," she says so she can continue her dreaming.

Sebastian, suspended in the vapors of his memory, resumes his narrative. . . .

"For over 400 hundred years the Vázquez's had imagined that Armando the Mariner had built the house of Martín Cortés in Mérida. But it was in northern New Spain, where the unconquered Indians lived, that he built the house so that the spirit could live amongst the freest of his Indian blood. That was how it happened, María Elena."

Fernando added a postscript:

Here ends the vision.

He looked at the clock. It was ten thirty in the evening. He changed his clothes and went to mass at midnight. When he returned home, he tried to sleep but undistinguishable echoes reverberated inside his ears. After several hours, he made another journal entry.

May 11th

Dearest Niece,

Even as I attended midnight mass, I was haunted by the night visions carried by the winds. The woman and man of the wind visions exchanged words and fluids of love, more in a synchronized dream than reality, as dim as shadows and as real as the impatient urge that once ran through my legs and never fulfilled manhood. Not because of God or Church, but because of my own timidity, certain of a woman's laughter at my own ineptness. Yet this woman of my stolen dreams articulated with her body the music of molecules and planets, dissolving her lover into his own secrets, words spoken in the cadences of birds, the watery movements of reptiles, man's escape of death through a woman's body. Lupita, perhaps your intuition was right all along, perhaps God can only gain our devotion when we are torn, incomplete, frustrated in the most simple expressions. For what is true divinity except the transcendence of the ordinary? Yet it is possible in that primitive act of love. And now, here in the solitude of my bedroom, through the open window, return the visions of never dreamed dreams, voices stolen by the restless winds.

The sun is beginning to rise, Lupe, but unlike other mornings when the voices vanish, María Elena has begun to speak. I can hear her saying. . . .

"This is the remembrance you must keep from the Trickster, Sebastian.

"It was long ago, before *Papá* sent you away, and you became the stranger I came to love. I had not even started school yet when you and Josesito took me with you to Mexico. It was my first time. The rest of you had your stories. It was from these

120

stories that I created the images of the Mexican desert and its Spanish villages, the tales retold from the old ones who still remembered the last of the Apache raids.

"Josesito had just bought a '64 Plymouth he planned to restore but never did. The two of you decided to drive to Mexico on a whim. You and he were going over the plans, and I was close by listening. From your remembrances I imagined that world, constructed a reality as if it were a dream. Then you asked me, 'Do you want to go with us, *amor?*'

"*Papá* and *Mamá* immediately opposed the idea, but Josesito interceded, 'Come on, *Papá*, she's the only one in the family whose never gone. Don't worry, we promise to take good care of her.'

"The next morning you woke me up at five o'clock. The two of you had decided to drive without stopping, and that was the first time I experienced the night in motion. I slept on the back seat while the two of you talked and smoked. The sounds of the engine and your voices and the motion upon the road entered into my sleep, became the primitive music of desire. When you stopped for gas or food, you would wake me and the liquidity of the night was broken by the artificial lights and the odors of spilt gasoline, the burnt air of the desert, the rotting fish stench of the bathrooms. Even the sound of English seemed an intrusion to the spell of the night and Spanish. It would be many years later, after I had learned the languages of the Indians, that I would come to realize that Spanish was my language of night and secrets.

"For two straight days, the two of you took turns driving, but at the beginning of the third night, even after a nap, the driver began to fall asleep at the wheel.

'It's best we pull off the road and sleep,' you said.

Josesito agreed. 'You're right. Better late than never.'

"Josesito slept in the front seat. You made a bed of pillows on the floor in the back for me so you could sleep on the back seat. I watched you sleep until I fell into a strange dream, as if I had been submerged in the green waters of a distant planet. After a while, I got cold and so I crawled next to you to get warm. Your warmth induced a wonderful dream. I was dreaming that I was still awake and the stars had come alive. When I opened my eyes, I knew I had been dreaming yet the dream had been real because the stars were now upon us, watching us. When they realized that I, too, was watching them, they returned to the perimeter of the sky. I then looked at you, and I felt at that moment a love foreign to my innocence. From that moment on, Sebastian, I was destined to love you.

"I remember the night of the border crossing in Piedras Negras. The Mexican immigration official kept insisting that I needed some immunization shots. Josesito was furious.

'I tell you the kid's had her shots. Here are her papers.'

The official's assistant, a tag-along without a position, pretended to read the papers and said we would have to wait until the morning so they could call the health department in California.

"Finally you said to them, 'See here, *Señores*, we have been driving for three days straight. Our relatives are waiting for us in Nava. Is there not anything you can do?'

"'I can expedite the paperwork, *joven*,' the official said, 'but that means I will be working without any pay.'

"You opened your wallet and handed the official a twenty dollar bill. Pleased, the official nodded, and the tag-along immediately began to load our luggage back into the car. You gave him three dollars, and as we pulled out of the station, Josesito rolled down his window and yelled towards the official and his stooge, 'I am going to kill you!'

"'Take it easy, Josesito' you said. 'Just forget about it.'

"'I hate those corrupt bastards!'

"'It's nothing. Let them take a little bite, and we can get on with things.'

"'Not right!'

"'Well keep your cool, *manito*, because they are going to nail us again at the *vientidos* substation.'

"At the substation, a fat immigration official waved us over with a flashlight. This time you got out by yourself. We could see you talking and the official nodding, appearing sympathetic. You handed him a bill, and he let us through. About thirty minutes later, we arrived in Nava. You seemed to turn the car into an empty space, and the *pueblo* appeared, as if it had been purposely hidden from the casual observer.

"There I saw the realization of my many dreams formed from the memories of my family. I rolled down the window and could hear the running water of a stream, the air pregnant with the voices of the storytellers

"Remember, Rising Eagle, so that I will not be ruined by forgetfulness. . . . I am dreaming, Cuauhtlehuanitl, that. . . ."

Fernando did not know if her voice had faded with the rising sun or if he had fallen asleep and neglected the end of her narrative. He was awakened at one in the afternoon by a concerned young priest, who, having not seen the old man all day, feared he had died in his sleep.

18

The Spanish Refugees

If it had not been for José's friendship with the son of a Mexican doctor, the Vázquez family would never have left Spain. Jorge, who disdained the Spanish capital, calling it a nest of fascists, worked hard along side his father, *Don* Gustavo, to send the younger brother, José, to the university in Madrid. It was there that José became friends with the doctor's son. While José was studying at the university, Jorge continued his involvement with an anti-government Leftist group. One evening, there was a fight in a bar, and a policeman was killed later that very night. Jorge Vázquez became the main suspect, although he always denied he killing the policeman. At the height of Jorge's troubles, José's friend's urged the Vázquez family to emigrate to Mexico. The friend's father was an official with the government in Mexico who could pull some strings through the Swiss embassy. Jorge, who was now in hiding, needed no further persuasion. The same could be said for *Don* Gustavo, who wanted to fulfill his ancestral fascinations with the New World. Only José resisted the idea, but with his mother dead, there was no one else to seriously oppose this suggestion. As the youngest son, he felt compelled to obey.

Once the decision was made, *Don* Gustavo wanted to go to Mérida because, according to family lore, their ancestor had supposedly built a house there for a ghost. But both the sons knew that beginning life in a new land was hard enough without chasing the hallucinations of their inherited dreams. 'To hell with that,' they thought, and the two sons decided between themselves to go to Monterrey in northern Mexico and start a business.

When the ship disembarked from Spain, *Don* Gustavo, took out a bottle of wine and proposed a toast with his sons, *"Viva México,* the land where the liberals defeated the Church-loving sons of whores."

Don Gustavo, an ardent Republican, prided himself in his liberalism. Through modest wealth and social position acquired by their ancestor Armando, the Vázquez's over the centuries had been hidalgos— middle-class farmers and small businessmen. But, perhaps, because of the remorse their ancestor had felt during the conquest of Mexico, they were always possessed of ideas that were more egalitarian than those of their neighbors.

They were also passionately anti-cleric, blaming the church for the backwardness of their countrymen and the injustices they perpetuated. *Don* Gustavo, after his grandchildren were born, relished recounting the story about how, in 1809, his great-great-grandfather had been one of many who had witnessed Colonel Lemanior's demolition of the Castle of the Inquisition in

Madrid, exposing the heinous crimes of the Church—unburied cadavers in various stages of decay that still displayed the agonized expressions of the tortured. The Vázquez's had been sympathizers of the first Spanish Republic in 1873 and in subsequent feuds, lawsuits and counter-lawsuits against their conservative, Carlist neighbors—many times over the most trivial matters—had brought themselves near financial ruin. By the time Gustavo married in 1922, his sole inheritance was a small butcher shop in Extremadura.

Jorge and José, who disliked their father's trade, made their own plans to open an import store in Mexico without their father's knowledge. They realized that the new rising Mexican upper class—one based on political affinities and alliance rather than blood—had a strong appetite for the fineries of Europe.

The brothers opened shop in Monterrey, Nuevo Leon, and became so successful that six years later, José, now married and with two children of his own, moved his young family and his father to California where he opened another store in San José.

Jorge Vázquez remained in Mexico and married a half-Indian woman. A year later, the contact between the brothers was abruptly, and some said mysteriously, cut off. Months went by, and José could not find any trace of his brother or sister-in-law. His persistence finally paid off when he learned that Jorge and his wife had both died, but had had a son. The boy was living with an old man who claimed to be his sister-in-law's father.

It was later discovered that Jorge Vázquez, who was

once as pragmatic and enterprising as his brother José, had been overtaken by the same hallucinating, inherited visions that were characteristic of the old man, their father. It was as if the Mexican desert had awakened in him some inexplicable desire to be absorbed by the silent Indian dreams. Perhaps, because he loved a half-Indian woman, he chanced to enter into one of her dreams by mistake and there saw in her night's memory a fragment of his own forgotten hereditary code, an emblem, a marker left by his ancestor, the Mariner Armando Vázquez.

José's business partner in Monterrey informed him that when his brother died, his brother's wife, pregnant and distraught over his death had disappeared and died later at her father's house. José returned to Mexico and found his brother's son living in poverty with an Indian named Pedro Eloy Joaquín, who claimed to be the boy's grandfather. The boy's fair complexion and his mariner blue eyes were all the evidence that José Vázquez needed to take the boy from the old man.

The boy's introduction into the family was difficult, for he was more comfortable with his Indian language than with the little Spanish he spoke. And what he did speak in Spanish concerned his adopted parents tremendously. "Crazy thoughts," they said.

It took numerous sessions with a priest—this at the urging of José's wife, Silvia—and finally a beating from José to convince Sebastian that he could not turn himself into a bird and fly. Henceforth, Sebastian retreated to the silent world of his dreams, constantly building little cities of rocks and scraps of wood in the yard and speaking softly to himself in what later was discerned to be the Indian language of his grandfather.

His other grandfather, Gustavo Vázquez, fascinated by the boy's Indian visions, told him the stories of Mérida and the old land grant and how their ancestor had been in love with Malintzín herself. Sebastian thus became the keeper of the memories of two peoples whose dreams seemed destined to meet in the violence of love and rebirth.

His adopted brothers, Ricardo and Josesito, who were older than he and preferred much more conventional diversions, ignored him as they had the grandfather. Only José's daughter Rachel, bored by the traditional restrictions on females, dared venture into Sebastian's self-created hallucinations and private mythologies. As if in a collective dream, the two would create an imaginary world in their games and felt as though they had actually traveled into their miniature cities. *Don* Gustavo would sit and watch them for hours, himself absorbed in their waking visions, recognizing in their mariner's eyes the ancient signs of the Vázquez dream.

19

Duty

Rachel Vázquez had a voice mail from her mother waiting for her when she returned from a business trip in Los Angeles.

"*Mi hija*, this is me. Please come to San José as soon as you can. Your brother Sebastian is not well and I need your help."

Without hesitation, she made the hour long drive from San Francisco to San José. Even in her middle age, she was still accustomed to obeying the wishes of her mother and, while he lived, her father. She always tended to the needs of her family, no matter how absurd, unlike her brothers, Ricardo and Josesito, who had separated themselves from Sebastian's difficult situation after the death of their father, *Don* José.

Their mother, *Doña* Silvia, who devotedly cared for Sebastian without complaint, had resigned herself to her adopted son's madness almost as if she had known it would eventually happen. Unlike her husband, she did not believe that Sebastian's fascination with Indian magic alone had caused his mental breakdown. To Silvia, it seemed as if God himself had willed Sebastian to a destiny of misfortune.

When all of the children were young, her own children would become jealous of her sentimental attention towards Sebastian.

"I feel sorry for the boy, *pobrecito* orphan," she would say. "He was born with the look of sorrow in his eyes. His mother must have wept constantly while she was pregnant."

José Vázquez, however, would not have any of that sentimentality shown in his presence. "You'll make that boy a weak *maricon*," he'd say.

José, although liberal for a man of his generation, nonetheless retained the values of the old ways. There were two things he would not tolerate: a woman's loss of her honor and a man's loss of his masculinity. Thus, he took his brother's son as if he were his own and fed him the same poisonous traditions. The boy, a stranger to the family, did his best to please his uncle-father, but he found true refuge with Rachel who was now his sister. The two, exactly the same age, became the best of friends, although after María Elena's birth they drifted apart. After Sebastian became afflicted with his mental illness, Rachel, out of her sense of duty, continued to see him, but she was ever irritated, for he, in his madness, revived memories that Rachel desperately wanted to repress.

When she arrived in San José, she asked her mother, "What's wrong with him?"

"He's been talking non-stop now for days," said Silvia.

"Talking with himself? On the phone? What?" asked

Rachel irritably.

"He talks into thin air, with María Elena and sometimes with you."

Rachel went upstairs to the small apartment over her mother's garage where Sebastian was staying. The door to the apartment was ajar and she could hear him talking.

"When you were born, no one knew what to name you. No one but I had thought about it. They wanted to give you some terrible name like Refugio, some name fit for a nun, but not for you. I could see it in your eyes, and I said to *Papá* José, 'We should name her after my mother.' And *Mamá* Silvia said it would be fine, that it was good to name children for those who have died so we may remember them. I wanted them to add 'Del Joaquín,' but they were scandalized that you would have an Indian sorcerer's name, so they just kept María and added 'Elena' because it was your great-grandmother's name.

"Later you would ask me if it was true that Pedro Eloy Joaquín, my other grandfather was a form-changer. 'Yes,' I told you. 'But you are an Aztec and a descendant of the Toltec dreamers. Your father was the re-born prince."

Rachel stepped into the room. "What are you doing, Sebastian? Answer me that, at least, or I'll lose my mind."

She found Sebastian huddled in a corner, shivering, naked except for a blanket.

"I'm waking up from a dream of the sea, Rachel," he said, his eyes pale from his perpetual pain. "I have come back from the past. I saw your lover there."

Rachel went to the closet and took out some clothes. "For the love of God, Sebastian, put these on."

"I'm seasick, Rachel. Please help me."

She helped him dress without any anger. She wanted so badly for him to be well, for although he was her cousin and adopted brother, she, in her heart, was always closer to him than her real brothers, Ricardo and Josesito. There was a time, during their adolescence, when they had been the best of friends, but now his insistence on rehashing the unpleasant memories of the past—her one and only indiscretion with a man who deceived her—put a strain on their relationship.

After she helped him, she soaked a towel in some ice water to use as a compress. She remembered how the cold compresses had helped him as a child when he had attacks of vertigo.

"You have to let go of the past, Sebastian," she said as she applied the cold towel to his forehead, cheekbones, and neck.

"I cannot let go of the past because I have already died, Rachel. Do you not remember you buried me yesterday?"

"Stop it, Sebastian! You know you're not dead."

"María Elena said I was dead. But she will bring me back to life when we go away."

"Sebastian," she said, gently. "You are not dead, and María Elena is not coming for you, ever. You've got to let the past go. You've got to let her go, so she can find some happiness, so that I can find some peace of mind."

Perhaps because Sebastian sensed the wounds in

Rachel's heart, or perhaps because she had implied that María Elena could find happiness without him, he became very quiet. Suddenly Rachel found the silence was more unnerving than his madman's rantings.

"What are you thinking, brother?" she asked after a while.

"About *Abuelito* Gustavo," said Sebastian pensively.

"What about him?"

"I was remembering one of the stories he told us about the old Mariner Armando Vázquez."

"Which story?" she asked, herself now infected by his melancholy.

"The one about how *Doña* Marina was in love with the Mariner, but Cortés gave her to another soldier out of spite to show he had power over them. Do you remember the story now, Rachel?"

"No, brother. I don't remember. What else happened?" She was relieved, that for at least this moment, he had reverted to his old, seemingly rational self.

"Marina and Armando made a secret vow to meet again in another world."

"Yes," said Rachel. "I remember now. . . . Sebastian, I have to go home now. Promise me you'll dress yourself from now on. You know it bothers *Mamá* to see you naked."

"Yes, I promise," he said. When she was about to leave, he said to her, "Remember the night when your lover became the king, how splendid he looked with his golden belt?"

20

Passion of the Spirit

The young acolyte was extremely polite. "Wait here one moment, Father Fernando, while I announce you to the Bishop."

He then momentarily disappeared, leaving Fernando Ocampo alone to once again ponder his present predicament. Fernando had no idea that his nocturnal excursions had aroused the superstitious suspicions of his immediate superior, Father Tomás, until he was told that the Bishop wanted to meet with him. He knew this was Father Tomás's doing. 'At my age, they think the only one who can exert authority over me is the Bishop himself.'

For the first time in his life, Fernando Ocampo was resentful towards the Church. Unlike many of his colleagues who viewed the holy calling as an economic opportunity, especially after the revolution when times were hard and food scarce, Father Fernando had given his soul and body unequivocally to the Church. While he sat in the Bishop's antechamber, in that eternal moment of waiting, Fernando remembered the other priests he had known in his lifetime. Most had merely gone through the motions, lived a life of ease, neglected the vow of chastity. Whenever he went home to Querétaro, he would hear rumors. *"Vino un padre, bien padre."* So said the young women whenever some handsome young priest was assigned to the parish.

But Fernando, in his entire life, had never violated his vow, never seen a woman's body, never savored a woman's embrace, never tasted a woman's oceanic-like skin, until the visions of the night brought him in proximity with the green-eyed stranger. It was as if he could feel the sensations of Sebastian's interactions with his lover through the remembrances that floated in the nocturnal airs. As he sat patiently in the elegant antechamber, the tips of his fingers still remembered the silk of her hair. 'They want to deny me even my dreams and my most secret mysteries. They no longer believe in mystery or miracle or the passion of the spirit. They—'

"The Bishop will see you now, Father," announced the acolyte, breaking Fernando's introspections.

When Fernando entered the Bishop's office, his senses suddenly magnified, as if his magical encounters in the night had increased his powers of sensual perception. The objects in the room emitted distinct odors, as though they were flowers. The old wooden furniture gave off the faint scents of extinct forests. The centuries old paintings radiated the organic ethers of medieval oils. Even the old books smelled of the exhausted and stale breaths of the once living priests who had pored over their texts. The invasion of so many odors began to nauseate Father Fernando. To divert his attention from his senses he focused on the fleshy, lethargic face of the Bishop.

The Bishop did most of the talking. Fernando did not deny the allegations. "Yes, holiness, I heard voices in the convent in Querétaro."

There were concerns, said the Bishop, that even obsessions with the mysteries of God could endanger one's immortal soul. Even something as innocent as taking a sleeping drug needed to be done in moderation. Excesses could invite the curiosity of the legions.

"The Devil disguises himself as an angel of light and may lead us, even in old age, to the temptations of the flesh," intoned the Bishop.

Fernando, upon hearing those words, repressed the urge to laugh, thinking, 'The old are too tired to sin.'

Unless dreams were real and reality a shadow of dreams. Because, as he sat in the Bishop's office, he could again feel the woman's body, the chaos of her green eyes, and his ears became filled with the music of her strange and elusive language. In the mist of his memory, he could almost understand her, but focusing on the immediacy of the moment at hand, her meanings vanished. But her name he remembered. María Elena. . . .

"Please do not misinterpret my concern, Father," continued the Bishop. "I and everyone who knows you respects you and your unfaltering work for the Church. It is because of our love for you that we are concerned. I suggest you limit your walks to daylight hours. These are dangerous times and even holy men can fall prey to criminals. Take some time to relax, Father, and use your medications with care. . . ."

The Bishop rambled on for another half-hour. Fernando remained silent and deferential.

"Many of our young priests and brothers look up to you, Father Fernando. We want to keep you here with us for a while longer before God calls you. But we do not want to see you fall into temptation after a lifetime of fealty."

"I will be careful, holiness," Fernando said obediently.

The Bishop was satisfied and sent him home. Fernando knew he had accomplished his goal of protecting his secret, but the meeting had left him humiliated and resentful. His inner peace was disrupted, his most secret gestures exposed to the scrutiny of the bureaucratic mentality of his colleagues. Agitated and unsettled, he found he had lost his capacity to penetrate the hidden frequencies of wind and dream. It was not until many nights after his meeting with the Bishop that he again heard her voice, and as if she could hear him, he said, "It is you María Elena. I thought you had forgotten me."

Fernando, lying on his bed, quickly took his journal which he always kept on his nightstand to document his vision. Feverishly, he wrote the words she spoke:

> "When you believed the spirit of your mother, Sebastian, you condemned me as an outcast to my family. I allowed myself to fall in love with you because *Papá* José had once said that you were not his brother Jorge's son. He lied about many things, but why would he believe that rumor unless there

was an element of truth to it? You always said that your mariner's eyes were the ultimate proof of your origins, but Pedro Eloy Joaquín told you that his wife was a Frenchman's daughter whose eyes were as blue as the distant seas. If you had rejected your claim to your Vázquez blood, I could have loved you, not as an outcast and traitor to my family, but as a normal woman. When you insisted on your birthright, I became obsessed with finding another way to be with you. We were both always drawn to the mysteries of the ancients. Sooner or later, you would come to me, ostensibly to learn the same mysteries, but really to be with me. That is the truth. Do not deny it, or has the sickness of the sea wiped your memory clean?

"Why did you keep the secret of my paternity away from me, Sebastian? How could you have known and never told me? I remember when *Papá* José exposed the secret. You had left again after coming for my *quinceañera*. His instincts told him immediately how I felt about you.

"'Tell me, yes or no, do you love your own brother in this filthy manner?'

"'Yes,' I told him. 'It is true.'

"It was as if he had lost his mind—I never told you the rage he felt. I was certain he would beat me. I expected it, welcomed it as a relief from the love I felt for you. I never expected what he was about to tell me.

"'My daughter, your mother, betrayed me by having you. You are her all over again.'

141

"The deathly pall that came over *Mamá* told me I had heard *Papá* correctly. At that instant, many thing became clear to me: why Rachel was distant with me, why the looks *Mamá* gave her could silence her. But, Sebastian, before that moment, I had no idea. I loved *Papá* and *Mamá* all my life with all of my devotion, but then the illusion was shattered. Strangely, it freed me. Who were they to ask that I not love you? They had broken the rules before me. Perhaps I was nothing more than all of their sins realized. But I could not free myself completely from them because they were the blood of my mother. And perhaps she had rejected me, but not *Papá* José and *Mamá* Silvia. You can only be sure of your mother's blood, Sebastian. How can you prove the rumors about your mother are untrue?

"But, beloved, I no longer care if you are my cousin. I would love you just the same if you were my brother.

"I saw you last night in a dream. You were wandering through a city in northern Africa. I asked what you were doing and you said you were sightseeing for Pedro Eloy Joaquín. 'When I meet him after I am dead, Joaquín will be able to read my eyes and see the ancient city,' you said.

"I don't want you to talk like that anymore. I am tired of not seeing you except in my dreams. Perhaps you should not have given me hope by loving me, but I wanted anything, even a false hope. It was only a matter of time before they found us out. When *Papá* went to Montemorelos to find us, the townspeople told him, 'She used to walk along the plaza every night with a *güero* who is her *querido*.'

"You should have spoken to me before you left me. I would have found a way to be with you like I did in Guanajuato. But now, all I have is your voice that returns to me in the cycles of the night. Give me your thoughts at the very least, beloved."

The walls in Fernando Ocampo's room appeared to melt. His eyes could see them in another time. The two of them had gone to the countryside, still obsessed with the cyclical mystery they had alluded to in the fragments of the conversations he had overheard. Fernando, as he watched the vision, wondered, why didn't they just run away together? Was there some inherited madness that made them chase the obsessions of their ancestor? A fatalistic fire burned inside of them, as if they were predestined for some apocalypse.

They consulted an old woman, an Indian fortune teller. The fortune teller swept them with a handmade broom, whispering a spell in a strange language. She sat before them, entranced in prayer, her eyes penetrating the visions that had disappeared in the currents of air centuries before. They watched the ancient woman's face to see if it revealed any emotion through its inscrutable mask of old age. But there was no change, no sense of wonder or abhorrence, only the words formed by her mouth, as though she were a recording machine repeating the commands of an unseen master.

"Your destinies have become intertwined," she

said. "Neither of you can separate yourself from
the other's hallucination. The madness of the desire that brought you together was a centuries-old
fate. It found you, loved you, destroyed your conti-
nuity, created a new possibility, forged the past into
a new dream.

"Long ago Malintzín dreamt of Queztalcoatl, yet
it was not a god but a white man from another
shore that she was destined to love. But she was not
a free woman. She could not say, 'I choose this
man,' and so the captain-general took her instead
of the one destined for her, a blue-eyed mariner.
The child she bore the captain-general should have
been the son of the Mariner, the man for whom her
heart secretly longed. They were never lovers but
they made a vow to each other, and unknown to
them this vow was destined to repeat in another
cycle of time. All things repeat: desire, histories,
migration of animals, heavenly storms born of
the nostalgia of stars.

"Desires are stronger than time, than the machines and forces of men. Our people said, many
years ago, that Malintzín would reappear and
that her son, Martín, would follow her. After the
return of the Iberians, Malintzín would find her
beloved Mariner again. Cuauhtémoc, seeing these
signs, would come out from hiding and free the
Indians from the yoke of the white man. All these
were separate destinies. One was to be Malintzín,
another was to be her son, Martín, another Cuauhtémoc, and still another the blood of the Mariner.

But all of these different persons have come together in this woman here." She pointed to María Elena. "You are the blood of Malintzín, and of Cuauhtémoc, and of the old Mariner. You have the eyes of Martín Cortés. What malediction or miracle made you one in the same with these others?"

"And you," she said to Sebastian. "You, too, are of the same blood of the Mariner. That is why you have sinned against your own flesh, because you were destined to find Malintzín again and love her."

The old woman turned her eyes to María Elena.

"Ah, you are not afraid. You are like your forefather, Cuauhtémoc. He was not afraid, not even when Cortés burned his feet. Perhaps Vázquez helped to burn the feet of Cuauhtémoc." The old woman laughed at the irony. "Desire is like smoke, an invader of air, a reminder that fire destroys but also creates. The heart of Martín Cortés was burned, the old rumors went, and the smoke of his heart infected the memory of generations. Our memory has survived time. We remember that the new cycle has come upon us, just as the last one came in the time of Moctezuma's grandfather. When the cycle turns, someone must take the place of Martín Cortés, die the ritual death, and pass into the chaos of the unseen.

"You," said the old woman to María Elena. "You are the one. You carry the mark of the condemned. You must die in place of Martín Cortés."

"And you," she said accusingly to Sebastian. "Your people are the form-changers from the desert. Don't you know the laws of your people forbid you taking a woman who is your kin? You must pay for your sins along with her."

María Elena reprimanded the old woman. "What you call sin is not sin but love."

Like a dream, the vision vanished, but María Elena's voice remained, speaking this time to Sebastian.

"After you went into your sleep spell of death, Sebastian, I lost hope of ever seeing you again and, disillusioned, I found someone else to love me, but I am betraying both of you because I cannot love either one completely. You wouldn't like him, that is, you wouldn't like him if you were my brother. . . .

"You are dreaming of the sea, and it is convulsing as if to vomit the ship into space. You are on it, and you are now at this moment saying, 'Release me, *amor!*' You want to step over the final border. It is at the edge of the sea, and there you will stop breathing and join the spirits of your dead, where it is peaceful. You want to take my place and die the ritual death intended for Martín Cortés. But I will not let you. No one must die. There was a time before the Olmecs when there were no sacrificial deaths. The fabric of space rips, exposing the multiple layers of the universe; time and space become one and the living can temporarily pass into another reality. That is the moment of a new cycle and it will soon arrive. The so-called myths are true, Sebastian. If you yourself have seen your grandfather Pedro change into the forms of animals, then you must know there are passages that open into the unseen chaos.

"But for now, I want you to remember those short three months when you and I were lovers, when we were in Montemorelos. Some Indians were holding a ceremony in town. They were singing praise to the old gods, and the houses built by the Spaniard stared at them in mute desperation, empty of the flesh of their builders, but still remembering the ancient chants of the exiles, songs that evoked the music of dreams. The song rose above the church, remember? We didn't dream it. The Indian songs that were once sung in secret now openly reached the Spanish colonia in the Mexican desert. The musical notes penetrated the adobe walls as the Indian bullets were never able to, like flying knives that awoke the dead. Only you and I could see them filing out of the cemetery: caballeros still in their war armor; ladies in their mantillas; and others, their bastard children too, looking at us, their brothers; and moments later, the dead spirits of the Indians, their wounds still bleeding, their tears not dried. But Martín Cortés was not among them. You and I asked the dead where he was, and they answered in a language no one could understand, but they knew. Later, we asked Pedro Eloy Joaquín what it all meant. But he only said, 'One of you choose and go with Martín, or he will take both of you. Renounce each other or die.' But I was already your lover. Now tell me your mariner's vision."

Fernando Ocampo heard Sebastian Vázquez answer her.

"I was aboard a large wooden ship. The ship sailed into the sea from a turbulent, muddy river. The spirits of the last Mexican prince Cuauhtémoc and *Don* Martín Cortés were looking for me and tossed the ship with their *brujos'* magic. And the sailors cried, 'Give the feathered ghost that man Vázquez!'

"*Querida*, I have written you many letters and destroyed them immediately thereafter because once the words are created they will reach you. I had never told you about your father, especially after we were separated. Neither of us needed the truth of reality at that time, but since we are now lost in this swirling sleep between death and silence, in this perpetual night that sounds like the rain, I will tell you the truth although there have been times when you have preferred lies. Not that I blame you, *amor*. The truth has always been a weapon used against you, used to confine you when, like me, you know the art of violating the prisons of this universe.

"I can teach you to fly, would you like that? I'll give you my magic of the eagle's flight although it has been forbidden to women. It is very simple, really, just lift yourself a little. When you catch the unseen currents, throw yourself into its power, then use the earth's gravity against itself, go downward to gain momentum and as you descend, catch an upward current and you will break away from the power of the planet. There is space in the center of the sky where you can travel freely and change directions at will. Do not be afraid, *amor*, I will go with you, and I will not leave you again. . . .

"You must forgive Pedro Eloy Joaquín for telling *Papá* José about us, *querida*. It was my mother's spirit that urged him to reveal our secret. She thought he could save us from a fate we wanted no salvation from. Like a good mother, she thought only of preserving her son, and from the other side of death, she, like many, forgot what it is like to love, how you do not exist until you abandon yourself in another. Or perhaps she remembered it too well and sought to preserve me because I was all that was left of her own love, not thinking of you, remembering only the ancient fate of Martín Cortés, thinking it something evil, when for us it was wonderful . . .

"When we went to Mérida in time for the vernal equinox, the spirits were roused from their sleep. The abandoned Vázquez mansion still echoed with its secret whispers, those betrayals waiting for retribution, desiring living witnesses. The blood of the Indians dripped from the cracks, crying out for relief and justice. They were still seeking their resting place in death. Robbed of their identity, they could neither enter their sacred resting place nor the Christian heaven, *amor*. They needed the blood of the last Mexican prince that runs in your veins to lead them to a resting place. All of the conquered dead clamored in that night, like the sound of a torrential rain. The ancient dead were waiting for you because I could not pay for Martín Cortés, and his ritual death was the ransom for their eternal rest. After I entered the sleep death, I paid for the sins of the Spanish soldiers, sacrificing the dried bones of the Mariner Armando Vázquez in a desert ritual. His burning bones wept for Martín, and it is you with your many languages who will learn the secrets of the conquered dead. You must enter a portal where many colors will swirl like the nebulas, and end this cycle of man.

"In your father Ramiro's veins ran the blood that could have freed them all. Perhaps if he had died in the ring during a fight, the cycle could have been completed, unknown and unseen by the world around him. But what did Ramiro care for the past? His ancestral memory was rendered inert by centuries of conquest. He wanted only to have glory, money, women, power to spit on others. He used to laugh at me when I told him the stories that *Abuelito* Gustavo had related to me: stories about the conquest; the blood of Indians that death could not silence; the guilt of Armando the Mariner, who could have killed Hernán Cortés and taken his woman, the Indian noblewoman Malintzín; how she pleaded for the life of the father of her son; how the Mariner foresaw the death of Martín Cortés and fled his hallucination by returning to Spain.

"'*Muchacho loco*,' said Ramiro, 'just a baby, but you're as senile as an old man. You got a girlfriend? You need a girlfriend. Time to become a man, *güero*.'

"But I knew he was the one. I could see him in his glory, the Indian prince transported from a different epoch. I went to his training sessions, watched his elegant body float in athletic genius. During the title match, it was as if he were supernatural. His opponent, another Mexican named Salvador Ontiveros, barely grazed him. Your father could destroy other men with dreams as large as his. But I told you that before, and you are impatient with me.

"After we were separated, I went and searched for your father. I found him in San Juan de Teotihuacán of all places. He has a little restaurant there. You may have even seen it, may have, during your work, gone in there and bought a cold drink and seen your brothers and sisters serving the customers. Isn't that ironic?

"I told him, 'Do you remember me, *Señor*?'

"He shook his head, 'I have met many people, but I have chosen to forget them. The past means nothing to me. It brings me only bitterness when I should be content. I was once the Lightweight Boxing Champion of the world and now I am a miserable man.'

"'I know about the championship,' I said. 'I was in San Francisco the night of the fight. I was only a kid. My name is Vázquez.'

"He then remembered me and seemed more delighted at the thought of his memory working than at seeing me. I told him about you but he seemed . . . I cannot find the words.

"'*Señor*,' he said. 'If just once a year all the children I made would come and visit me and buy a cup of coffee or a soda at my cafe, I'd be a rich man.'

"I had expected him to be more curious, or to recall exactly the woman, your mother, that he had been with.

"'So what was it? Boy or girl?' he asked coolly.

"'Girl,' I said. 'She is grown now, an archeology graduate student at a school in Pennsylvania.'

"'Good,' he said without much interest. 'It's good that I did something right.'

"I am sorry. I had hoped that he would at least remember your mother's name.'"

"So it was him!" said Fernando Ocampo out loud. "Ramiro Huerta!"

Silence ensued, as if his outburst had frightened away the voices of the night currents. Fernando remembered again the time, twenty-seven years before, when Ramiro won his world championship in San Francisco. Fernando's brother, Juan, had come to Mexico City to watch the fight on closed circuit television. He had invited Fernando to attend the event, but the priest refused. Having seen Ramiro abuse his niece Alicia, he harbored no well-wishes for him and secretly wanted to see him not only lose, but take a bloody beating. But he suspected that Ramiro would win, and he did. The next day, Juan Ocampo collected the tabloid newspapers for Fernando.

Fernando got up from his bed and took an ancient, bulging scrapbook from his bookshelf. Carefully, he laid it on the bed and sat down and began to turn the pages. 'Maybe I saved them,' he said to himself.

And then, there they were. "Huerta defeats Ontiveros!" screamed the headlines. There were also pictures published from his training camp. In the background was his entourage, among them a sixteen-year old boy. The orange-brown tinged photo showed his eyes to be a clear shade. In another photograph, Ramiro was shown at a party with a blond, young woman with the same clear-shaded eyes.

"So it is them!" said Fernando of the two young people in the photograph. "Sebastian and María Elena's mother!"

Fernando tried to delve further into this memory, imploring the winds to reveal more but instead he saw. . . .

People from another time. Fernando knew that these whom he saw were the dead, because unlike his visions and voices of María Elena and Sebastian, which emitted waves of warm reds, purples and oranges, the voices of the dead were hollow and smoky, and their images like a pestilent cloud of gray insects.

Surrounded by what seemed to be the walls of a medieval castle, a middle-aged man was training an adolescent boy in the military arts. Engaged in swordplay, the man pushed the boy hard. But at the end of the lesson, he affectionately embraced him. The two sat together, ate and drank.

The boy spoke first.

"Why are you not like other men, *Don* Armando?"

"How is that son?" asked the man.

"Other men, like my father are drunk with their own glory. Why not you? I hear you were given as much glory as the rest. Why are you so modest?"

"Only God knows, Martín."

"I have been listening to the stories of my father's comrades. *Don* Bernal Díaz says you were my mother's bodyguard."

"Yes, son, I was her protector."

"I heard that you were in love with her, *Don* Armando" said Martín.

"Who told you that?" asked Armando.

"Juan Jamarillo the younger, my half brother. He said his father won her over you."

"Your father gave her to the gentleman, Jamarillo, Martín, but she loved me, swore it to me."

The boy became uneasy and suspicious. "Swear by the holy cross, *Don* Armando, who is my father? You or the Captain-general?"

"The Captain-general, by the holy cross and the blood of our Lord. I never touched your mother. I only dreamed of her and still do. Even my children claim to have seen her in their dreams."

"Why did my father take her in the first place if he knew? He could have had any other woman."

"Her beauty and her many languages, Martín, that is why."

"I've heard it said that she could interpret the language of dreams, that she was a diviner among her people."

"Yes, it is true. But her gifts were from God, not the angel of darkness, Martín. She saved our lives many times over."

"My half-brother, Juan, calls you the Mariner, and so does *Don* Bernal. Why?"

"Your mother gave me that name because she said the I had the distant oceans in my eyes. . . ."

"Martín!" A man with an long beard called him.

"At your orders, *Papá*," said the boy.

"Come. . . ."

"It was him! Ramiro Huerta!" Father Fernando was startled by the bitterness of his own voice.

21

The Geography of Memory

They lived in the virtual silence of unrecognized neighbors. Months had gone by since Manuel Muñoz had brought María Elena home with him. Frustrated that he could not intuit her meanings and intonations, María Elena ceased all attempts to communicate with him. Whenever he asked her a question, she merely gestured "yes" or "no" by nodding or shaking her head. Even his most affectionate attempts to distract her were met by a melancholic disregard.

Whereas in the beginning of her convalescence she had tried speaking to him in her obscure Asiatic language, she now made no effort at all. Instead, he would hear her at night, speaking into the winds or humming melodies in her sleep. The sensual tones of her voice deeply disturbed him. If he had not been watching her and merely overhearing her, he could swear that she sounded as if she were with another man. Doubts began to invade his thoughts. Who was she, really?

Deprived of conversation, Manuel Muñoz was forced to rely on his memories of the María Elena he had known, rather than the one who now resided with him as if she were an embodied ghost. Her solitude was now total and impregnable, as absolute as a recent memory. Her distance did not so much anger him as it made him sad. As much as he tried to repress the thought, her silence reminded him of the impossibility of owning her, that she was, and would be, never truly his. She had never agreed to marry him, she had only said, "If he says so, it must be true."

Against his wishes, she returned to work two and a half months after she was released from the hospital. Her doctors insisted she remain close to the city in case her condition worsened. They restricted her activities to locations in Mexico City and to the laboratories, where she concentrated on reconstructing artifacts. Manuel insisted on driving her to work and back home, unconvinced of her mental capabilities. Once in a while, when he lingered in her lab, her eyes would meet his and instead of resignation, Manuel imagined he saw her pitying him. Something in his imaginings told him it was that: pity and never love. He knew that in his neglected memories he would find her true feelings for him. As he retraced his memories, he began to decipher the self she hid behind her silence.

Manuel remembered how once, out of jealousy, he accompanied her to the Indian village of Palenque. Like many archeologists, she had been trained as an anthropologist and would many times engage in searching through the memories of the villagers for clues to the fragmented past. The ties she had established as a graduate student in the heart of the Mayaland had repeatedly brought her back to this village, where the elders arranged meetings with other elders from the neighboring villages and even from Guatemala. She would spend days patiently listening to the Indians as they repeated the same stories and events over and over. Once Manuel overheard her telling a colleague her theory on the nature of conversations, that the manner of the re-telling disclosed something in and of itself, as if the very structure was its own narrative. Rather than try to reconcile the differences in the stories, as a historian would, she looked upon the contradictions as revealing many, if not simultaneous, truths. She repeated this explanation to Manuel to ease his annoyance with her trips into the region, but instead his unmasked boredom with her work made her resentful and even less willing to confide in him.

Her numerous excursions into remote parts of the country caused something of a stir in Manuel's inner circle. Some of his friends remarked that she was a strange woman, so beautiful yet so resigned to living in the past. "Everyone has his work, but hers is an obsession," remarked one of his friends.

Manuel asked her once why she was obsessed with the past.

"Have I not told you that my ancestor loved Malintzín herself?" she said. "I am searching for the answer to a mystery that plagues my people."

Manuel never bothered to ask her what she meant. He was satisfied with the illusion that he owned her.

But now, in the exile of silence, Manuel re-lived his memories, investigating their past life together much as she had searched the past for her so-called mysteries.

In those times when he was pursuing her, he had shown up at various archeological sites and had seen her interact with her fellow professionals. But seeing her for the first time alone with the Indians surprised him. María Elena was as at ease in that primitive world as she was in the modern. She spoke to them so naturally and fluidly, her gift, he remembered now. It never occurred to him that perhaps her multilingual abilities were related to her ailment.

Manuel's remembrance momentarily drifted back to his friends, and how they had perceived his romance with María Elena and teased him about it. Even if the bantering was good-natured, it affected him. In it, he detected a malice he himself had engaged in before becoming involved with María Elena. The implication was that a woman could never free herself from the jealousies of men, that she was an object of desire they secretly wanted to destroy because she reminded them of the possibilities of passion that they would never obtain unless they reciprocated by surrendering to a woman. These were men who reduced love to an empty game of honor or malevolent conquest. But it was the woman who was to be the conquered one and, thus, when they called him "Manuelito, *el conquistado*," they were seriously insulting him. They would say of the young archeologist, "She is a student of man. You are her subject."

Manuel had angrily endured the stupid comedy of his friends, knowing that once she married him, the nonsense would stop. Only then would he be able to rest under the scrutiny of a moral code that never preserved morality and merely invited its violation. Once she married him, he had planned to pressure her to have a child and, thus, coerce her to quit her profession. Under those conditions, he believed he could have easily controlled her drifting from him in her perpetual silent daydreams.

The trip to Palenque especially stood out in his memory because, during that experience, he felt as if his dreams were invaded by the thoughts and dreams of others. María Elena had insisted on driving herself. She drove, without talking, through that ancient rainforest that seemed to have devoured the world and stood as a companion to memory, a portal to another planet. He lapsed in and out of sweaty naps. For fleeting moments he would feel the suffocating sensation that precedes a nightmare. He would force himself to wake up, but the hot jungle sun, as it poured through the windows, oppressed his resolve not to dream even as he turned up the air-conditioning. He fought to retain control of his senses and maintain his rational equilibrium.

In the brief dreams, interrupted by his efforts to stay awake, he saw María Elena in what seemed to him to be episodes of her life. As a child, he had been told once by his grandmother, that when we deeply love another person, we can begin to see inside the other's mind when we dream. What he had seen that day, unknown to him, was exactly that: the images of her mental wanderings as they materialized along the highway, like fragmented scenes from a movie. There along the road, for a micro-instant, Manuel dreamed her ancestral memories: from the windows of old Hispanic relics, he saw the faces of

161

blue-eyed men; emerging from the springs, naked boys as majestic as Aztec princes. Also, there were downcast women on their way to mass who,when they looked at him, resembled María Elena, as if she had been stolen from him and thrown into this nightmare of illusion; a procession of the dead that dwindled as it moved, as if its mourners too were taken into death by their motion; a man on horseback, followed by a black dog, the man's green eyes moving as the ocean's forgotten tides, his memory spurred by his constant motion.

The roadside hallucinations made Manuel sick. María Elena took him to a house in the village that belonged to some of her friends. There she left him to sleep off his motion sickness. It would not be the last time he would dream her memories, although that was the first. There, in the jungle, it seemed as if the primitive surroundings provided relief from his perpetual insomnia. He slept for many hours, and in his sleep, he overheard the voices of the Indians as they conversed with María Elena. He listened to the song-like cadences of their tongue that sounded as if it were the light that shone through broken clouds. And then she, María Elena, spoke as if that ancient sound were born on her tongue. Just as suddenly, another dialect would begin, like a river breaking into the currents of the sea. (He would later learn that Indians from different regions had agreed to meet María Elena on that night.) Again María Elena's voice would alter into another language as easily as an instrument can play different songs. Her languages changed several times and Manuel dreamt of *Doña* Marina, the elegant lover of Cortés.

After a while, Manuel forced himself out of the suffocating sleep and went outside where María Elena continued her conversations with the Indians. He noticed, suddenly, how much she resembled them, her dark skin blending into the darkening day. Still, she stood out amongst them like Malintzín, the exiled royal daughter returned through time, and it seemed as if she were saying, "I have survived my exile, I do not condemn you." Suspended in that moment of waking before dreams entirely vanish, he felt himself spiraling into another coherence, that if it took hold, could doom one to an exile from the world of modernity and reason. In that murmur of the ancient tongues, Manuel seemed to somehow comprehend and could almost anticipate their thoughts.

'Perhaps, a man hears strange murmurs before he goes insane,' thought Manuel as he rehashed the memory.

His mind again drifted back to Palenque. He remembered how he roused himself out of the dream spell and went to a well to wash himself of the sickly perspiration that clung to his skin. A woman came up to him and said something in Nahuatl inflected as a question, "Are you Malintzín's captain?"

An old desert *brujo* said in Spanish, "No, he's not the captain. Cortés is dead."

For the rest of that evening in Palenque, Manuel watched María Elena transform herself into another woman, one escaped from the collective memory of the Indians, as if she were the incarnation of their dreams.

He began to wonder, through the veil of his remembrances, if perhaps time itself were merely an imaginary division of nothingness. He had always equally considered the existential and mystical philosophies to be rubbish. But what if they were, even partially, true? Perhaps there existed a limbo where this woman he knew as a silent archeologist became a woman no longer defined by the conventions of their society, but rather, an independent entity, free of him, of the ridicules of sexual conventions.

Manuel remembered how later that night in Palenque he had drifted into a remarkable dream. He was astonished because he did not even realize he was sleeping. He had returned from a brief walk, and María Elena was already asleep. He lay next to her and, in an unrealized moment, he began to dream of her.

In his dreaming he saw her as perhaps ten years younger, about 15, and she was washing some dishes near a well in a northern village, somewhere in the desert. A boy with the mariner's blue eyes kept asking her to play a game with him and she refused as she was busy working. Then, in that strange logic of dreams where one suddenly finds himself in a different place, Manuel began observing the body of a man laid to rest inside an old abode house. A single mourner sat next to the body, and the mourner's dog lingered in the shadows. The room began to fill with the sound of women weeping which seemed to surround the mourner in a prison of noise. The smoke of the kerosene lamps filled the darkness with the suffocating perfume of a dying machine, and the night became impenetrable, as if the sun itself had died suddenly. Manuel's dream shifted again and he saw María Elena outside weeping, but now she was a grown woman, as he knew her. The boy with the mariner's eyes watched her silently, at a distance where she could recognize him. She turned and saw him and said, "I'll play the game with you now if you promise not to die." The boy turned suddenly and ran away. She ran after him and just as she was about to catch him, he turned himself into a bird and disappeared into the darkening blue of the night sky.

Manuel then awoke and heard María Elena weeping in her sleep.

Now, months after her accident, he thought, 'I should have woken her and asked her what she was dreaming that night. At least I would have her words to help me make sense of this memory.'

More than ever, with María Elena deep in the throes of her language madness, Manuel began to realize that words, despite their ambiguity, create boundaries of meaning. With silence, all meaning is possible, and it was this silence that drove Manuel Muñoz to words more than ever. He took whatever words he had, those stored carelessly in his memory and those he invented for María Elena as his salvation from her silence.

He could have left her after her disease of non-language afflicted her. No one would have blamed him. "*Pobrecito*, how can a man make a life with a crazy woman," his friends were saying behind his back. But somehow he became increasingly fascinated by the possibilities of silence. He would re-enter every memory, explore its geography for details he had left out, re-interpreting old conversation, inventing new meanings or perhaps he was merely discovering the true identity of reality.

One night, while María Elena was dreaming next to him, he went over his memories again:

It was the first time he had gone to California. Despite the fact that the Vázquez's were taken aback by the announcement that he and María Elena were engaged, they nonetheless had a small dinner party so that the family and Manuel could become acquainted. Manuel met all of María Elena's siblings and their spouses and children, everyone from her inner, familial circle save one—Sebastian. None of them spoke of him or apologized for his absence. Manuel knew he should have been there—or at least been accounted for—because María Elena had spoken of him and mentioned that like the rest of her family, he lived in Northern California. When Manuel asked for him, each family member said, as if they had conspired to give an identical response, "He's out of town."

Manuel decided to indirectly approach Silvia Vázquez about Sebastian. He sensed she would respond to his overture since she alone radiated feelings of good will towards him, unlike José Vázquez and his sons Ricardo and Josesito, who seemed to harbor a thinly disguised resentment, as if they knew he had been intimate with María Elena and could almost sense his touch upon her skin.

During the gathering, when Silvia came to offer Manuel a drink, he asked her to describe the photographs on the mantle, those of her children in various stages in their lives. He began by asking about Rachel's photograph, taken at the time of her college graduation. Her square, elegant jaw, dreamy blue eyes, and melancholic expression reminded him, he told Silvia, of the Mexican movie actresses of the 1950's. That remarked please her, and she opened up to him.

"She and María Elena look a lot alike, don't they?" said Silvia. "Although María Elena takes somewhat after my own mother who was also olive skinned with green eyes."

"Who is this one?" asked Manuel of the photograph of Sebastian, feigning ignorance since he had seen the very same photograph in María Elena's office.

"This one," said Silvia sadly, "this one is my brother-in-law's only son, Sebastian. His parents died long ago, and my husband and I have raised him as our son. He has always been an equal to my children."

"In what place was this picture taken?" asked Manuel, remembering he had never asked María Elena about the strange, antiquated brick structure in the background.

"Pueblo Bonito in New Mexico. He likes the old Indian ruins and visits them frequently."

As if she divined what Manuel was seeking to learn, she excused herself, saying she had to begin preparing dinner and said nothing more of her nephew.

Only later did he learn the truth from Roberto Peña, Rachel's husband, who, visibly drunk, began to divulge Sebastian's whereabouts.

"You really want to know where Sebastian is? GONE!" Roberto's intoxicated state made him grotesque and idiotic, whereas a few hours earlier while sober he had been gentlemanly and sophisticated.

"Gone to New Mexico with his crazy Indian relatives. But what the hell, he's crazy, too. They'll do one of their little *brujeria* things. . . ." He stopped when he saw Rachel walk into the room. "Ah, here's the boss," he said stupidly.

Why hadn't he caught on that Roberto was not using a figure of speech, that Sebastian was, indeed, mad? Perhaps madness, like a country, exists in a geography unseen to all except the mad. Perhaps Sebastian had bewitched María Elena into madness. But why?

At that point Manuel thought he heard a rooster crowing, but had actually dreamed it because he had fallen asleep while remembering. The sun had not yet risen but a dull grayness had replace the night. He closed his eyes again and began to dream of a castle near a green ocean.

In the dream, Manuel knocked on the gate of the castle, and soldiers, bearded men in sixteenth century military dress, emerged and spoke in unison, as if they were a choir. The thoughts spoken were of the leader who stood in the front, a dark man with piercing green eyes. His soldiers were young men he had captured, men who had tried to escape the sorcerer captain by swimming out into the sea, but the captain's magic commanded the water and brought them back. In the castle was a woman and she. . . .

In his dream, the rooster crowed again and Manuel was startled out of his sleep. María Elena appeared to be struggling inside her dream. He touched her, and she opened her eyes and spoke to him in Spanish, as if she were still speaking in her dream and he had just entered into her distorted world.

"If we make him think we are with him, we can make our escape!"

"Wake up!" he said frightened.

Her eyes clarified as the world of dreams melted, but her Spanish language remained long enough for her to say, "I was having a nightmare, Manuel. I was Martín Cortés's prisoner inside a castle. He had changed me into a man so I could fight, but Pedro Eloy Joaquín had changed me back into a woman. I was trapped in the captain's castle. . . ."

And her language dissolved into incomprehension.

22

Mexico City, 1568

The heads of the king's traitors were rotting in the *Zócalo* as the Inquisitors lead the bastard Martín Cortés to the prison. "No one is with me," he said to deaf ears, "no one is for me. My sin is to be who I am."

The eyes of the *Criollos* and the Indians alike watched him with repulsion and fascination. Half-breed: a scourge upon both their people. A visible reminder of a forbidden fornication, carrier of his father's name and his mother's memory. His parents were the destroyers of a world and, in this great city of the watchful gods, there needed to be blood spilled to reclaim the gifts of the sun, the fruits of the earth, and the calm of the recent dead. The Aztec priests had received a prophecy in their secret rituals: the blood of a great mixed blood warrior could satisfy the thirst of the hidden gods of the city and could pay for the new cycle of life. The defeated Aztecs were secretly glad that the inquisitors and the *visitador* Muñoz Carrillo had found the elder Martín Cortés, the decorated war hero, because they could not openly sacrifice the *mestizo* warrior, the son of the conqueror. His death would pay for the indiscretion of both races—Iberians and Indians alike—because he was the child of their illicit union.

He disappeared for days in the torture chambers. His cries were carried by the wind and entered every home and invaded the sleep of the city dwellers. "For the love of God! I cannot tell you what I don't know!"

Everyone hoped that he would die quickly and honorably as the Tlaxcatecan warriors had died on the altar of the Huitzilopochtli. But that was not to be. He was tortured for days, and the last that the city dwellers were to see of him was the morning he emerged from the prison en route to Spain. The people were happy that his wife and children had already fled the city so they did not have to see how his beauty had been destroyed. The Indians were weeping because he would not be allowed to die in his homeland, and the gods would never be appeased until they received the *mestizo* blood of a warrior in sacrifice. They knew that centuries would pass and there would be no hope for freedom; they knew they would pass into death without a resting place for their spirits.

None of them heard him speak to the Indian boy who was harnessing the mules on the wagon on which the prisoners were to be transported. "Quick tell me the inquisitors' names."

"There are many, *su merced*," said the Indian, a young boy of 15.

"The ones who tortured me, boy."

"They say. . . . "

A Spanish soldier shouted at the boy to hurry up.

"Some men named Muñoz, Velázquez. . . ." he whispered before the Spanish soldier returned with another prisoner.

"Remember those names, boy," said Martín Cortés. "Because I will come for them and avenge myself."

The night after the exile of Martín Cortés, the Aztecs secretly gathered at the Avenue of the Dead, in the deserted, ancient city of Teotihuacán. A procession of worshipers moved in the liquidity of silence. As the moon rose over the city, the high priest called out, "Teotihuacán, city of eternal possibilities. Although alive, we have commended our spirits to your hidden bowels. We have all met here after our death which is not yet our death. Remember tonight, these movements of blood and our secret thoughts, our unavenged suffering. Hear our thoughts and preserve our memories. Brother wind, devour our voices and send them through the barriers of time so that our progeny will remember us."

After the high priest had spoken, the members of the procession spoke their minds, their separate thoughts mingling with those of the high priest. A fifteen-year old boy among them kept repeating the names, "Muñoz, Velázquez, Muñoz, Velázquez, Muñoz, Velázquez. . . ."

He spoke the names in a musical rhythm, and others picked up his litany, with one unintended misinterpretation. They spoke into the night and created a wind that whispered, "Muñoz, Vázquez, Muñoz, Vázquez. . . ."

The priests, however, did not give up so easily. Years

later, the Water Sorcerers of the old gods conspired with a heretical Jesuit to arrange for the return of the remains of Martín Cortés to his homeland. True to his word, the aging priest finally delivered to them an urn filled with what was believed to be the ashes of Martín Cortés. They promptly, and secretly, buried it inside the Pyramid of the Magician in Uxmal.

23

Lupe Huerta

Guadalupe Huerta, called Lupe or Lupita by her family and friends, decided one Saturday morning that, rather than call her friends and go to the movies, she would instead visit her great-uncle Fernando Ocampo. While her mother still lived, Lupe had not been close to him because she had never felt close to God. 'How could I?' she thought, especially after watching her mother suffer at the hands of her father, his womanizing and drinking, his constant humiliation of a woman he had vowed before God to honor. 'Where is God in all of this?' she had wondered even as a child, 'Is God just, or does he merely use men to make women suffer so that they turn to him, so that he may have the devotion of the wounded?'

It seemed unfair to Lupe and so she had told her great-uncle about her feelings at her mother's funeral. Father Fernando—whom she regarded as a kind but confused man because he claimed that the Cathedral was inhabited by ghosts and that the wind was filled with voices—dismissed her rebellion as grief.

Still, with her mother now gone, Lupe began to

embrace the old priest. What at first was mere formality grew into a genuine relationship. With every visit, inexplicably, they grew closer. Even so, she had no idea Father Fernando was writing a manuscript for her filled with the strange narratives he heard in the currents of winds and dreams. Only later, after she read the journal, would she understand that the two shared a rare intuition, an insight into events that on the surface seemed irrational if not ridiculous.

For the time being, she knew of no logical reason for the deepening love between them. It certainly was not sentimentality. No, her father's cruelty had killed sentimentality in her and had also killed her sense of hope. Because of her despair, she came to consider the world an accident of physics and life a cruel joke of God. Had her father recognized her intellect and had her educated, she would have been a philosopher, meeting other young, brilliant minds. She had often prayed to God, when she was a child, that there be another who was more fortunate, but who was like her, her double, and it was because she suspected God had granted her that wish that she did not entirely become an atheist.

It was this very subject that was on her mind when she visited Father Fernando.

"I want to tell you something rather strange, uncle," she said. "I have never spoken to anyone about this,"

Lupe began by recounting how she remembered his supernatural assertions—the voices that floated in the Cathedral—on the day of the strange earthquake in the Yucatán, for she had never heard of such a disaster in that region of Mexico.

She was sweeping the patio in her father's restaurant in San Juan de Teotihuacán when her favorite show on the radio was interrupted by the news of the earthquake. Disasters had intrigued her since she was a child. Several Protestant sects, in their efforts to sway the faithful from the mother Church, had often predicted the end of the world. But of all those who had prophesized the end, the one Lupe vividly remembered was an old Indian sorceress, a woman the people called La Nahua, who had once cured her older brother of a fever. La Nahua had told Lupe that one day the spirit of Martín Cortés, the bastard son of the Captain-general, would free itself during an earthquake, and the world's end would be near. Although she did not fully understand what the old woman meant, Lupe was nonetheless fascinated and never forgot La Nahua's words.

"The spirit of Martín Cortés will return as an avenging warrior, yet he will not be seen except by those who carry the blood of the ancient sorcerers and Dreamers. For the rest, life will go on as if nothing has happened. But the world of the Indians shall be reborn in secret rituals," the old woman had told Lupe.

All of this Lupe remembered when the earthquake in the Yucatán occurred. She learned from the news broadcasts that several members of a team of archeologists from the State University of Pennsylvania and The National Institute of Anthropology and History were on site during the earthquake. More horrifying to her was that one of them was trapped inside the great Pyramid of the Magician in Uxmal.

Like many Mexicans, Lupe was fascinated by this

encounter with death. She followed the progress of the searchers and watched the rescue efforts on the newscasts. Three days later, the buried archeologist was found—still alive. Lupe hoped the television camera could get a picture of him, to see what a man would look like after being buried alive.

Then, what? There was the image, as she had hoped. Lupe was astonished to see that the archeologist was a woman, one not much older than herself. The attitude of the unburied woman reminded Lupe of the paintings of martyrs in the churches, a look of willful resignation to a horrific death.

"That was when I began to believe there could be a God," she said to Father Fernando.

"Why? Because of the strangeness of the events?" Fernando spoke pensively from his penitentiary of contemplation.

"Yes, uncle. Because I had prayed to God that there be another like me, and that other was the woman inside the pyramid," said Lupe.

Father Fernando, shaken by her insight, remained quiet but was thinking, 'Ah, she can see it, too! The mysteries that the winds proclaim! Somehow she knows!'

"I know that may sound fantastic, Uncle," she said rather anxiously. "But wait until I tell you the rest."

Lupe continued, "Some time ago, a man came into the restaurant looking for *Papá*. He was the brother of a woman who had had a child by *Papá* when he won the championship."

At that moment Fernando thought, 'That damned

boxing title. A man thinks he is a god when it is God who has given him the day."

"I believe," continued Lupe, "that the woman in the pyramid is my father's daughter, the one I had prayed to God for and, Uncle, I have seen her before in Teotihuacán. There were some archeologists as usual, and some of them came into the restaurant for drinks. There was a young woman with them. She spoke to some in French and others in English and to us in Spanish. She was like a magician with her tongue. My mother, may she rest in peace, said, 'It is good to see a woman like that to prove we are intelligent, too, not just something men can trample.'

I felt proud of her, too, but jealous because she wasn't much older than I and she was someone important and I was nothing—a girl who worked for her father. And at that moment I really hated my father because he sent my brothers to school, they who cared nothing for education, and he deprived me. *Mamá* would say to him, 'Ramiro, send Lupita to school to learn something. She is so bright.' And *Papá* would say, 'She does not have to go to school to learn to clean and have children.' And, Uncle, seeing the woman brought joy and sorrow into my heart and I damned my father for being so cruel.

"When they left, I noticed she had left a notebook under the table. I picked it up and ran after her. She was already driving away but saw me in her rearview mirror and came back. '*Señorita*,' I said, 'you forgot this.' She looked at me, not special, but not as some people do who think they're better than others. No, she looked at me the same way she had her important friends and said, '*Muy agradecida.*' There was something about her, a familiarity, a strange recognition, like seeing yourself in a mirror after you wake up from a long dream."

"What makes you think that this woman is your father's daughter?" asked the priest.

"The stranger who came to see my father said that my father's child was a daughter and an archeologist," said Lupe.

"That could be mere coincidence. How can you be so certain?"

"I know it in my heart, *Padre.*"

"You have not addressed me as '*padre*' since you were little. How long has it been since you have confessed?"

Lupe pondered for a while. "I was sixteen. So there you have it: I doubted the existence of God until the appearance of my father's daughter. . . . What's the matter, Uncle, you have a faraway look on your face."

"Oh nothing, really. For some reason, I was remembering some of the confessions I've heard. Some strange things are said, perhaps because we can be more honest with strangers than with our intimates. Perhaps . . . perhaps only old age can redeem our sins because the old lack the energy to sin."

"That is a wise thing you have said, Uncle."

He did not tell her that those words were once spoken to him by a sinner.

24

Vox

One day, weeks later, María Elena began to regain her languages. At the time, Manuel Muñoz was in the midst of preparing for a conference on international trade laws in Cancún. As a matter of course, given the conditions under which they were living, he informed María Elena that she was to stay with his sister while he was gone. Furious at the implication—that she was mentally incompetent and required constant supervision—she blurted out a protest half in Spanish and half in French. She knew instantly from Manuel's reaction that he partially understood her. From that moment on, she began to recover her languages. But, for nearly seven days, whenever she spoke, her sentences were always hybrids of her many languages.

Before he left, Manuel had her examined by the same psychiatrist who had first diagnosed her condition following her accident. The psychiatrist concluded that she had been afflicted by a rare form of amnesia. Although he could not find any precedent in the medical literature, his analysis was more plausible and acceptable than the assertion that María Elena's languages had been stolen by a spirit.

Despite the doctor's assurance that María Elena was well enough to be left alone, Manuel insisted that she stay with his sister as planned.

"C'est jealousy de tu parte!" said María Elena in her language fusion. Nonetheless, because she disliked quarreling so intensely, she capitulated and agreed to stay with Manuel's sister.

Manuel was stung by her accusation. It was true he was jealous, but this time his motives were based on his innermost fears. His intuition warned him of some unknown danger. He dared not tell her that recently he was haunted by a strange sound like the buzzing of insects or the hum of a primitive machine. Every so often, when he least expected it, the sound would clarify, as if it were a radio signal, and he'd hear his name. *"Muñoz, Muñoz , . . ."* chanted by a choir of lost voices.

During one of his naps, he again dreamed of the Indian sorcerers with green and white paint on their faces, and saw himself pursued until an earthquake devoured him. In another dream: a gentleman—a *caballero*—from another era, dressed in black, sighted him in a crowd. The *caballero* gestured Manuel to follow him. *"Ven, Muñoz, ven. . . ."*

Manuel began to vaguely remember a story his grandmother had once told him as a child. What was it? A priest accompanies a man through a journey in the wilderness. The disembodied hand of the Devil pursues the man. *"Ven, ven, . . ."* they would hear the devil say.

What else? What did the man do to deserve this? The priest performs a ritual. The man steps outside the house and is seized by the devil.

Following his successful conference in Cancún, Manuel drove to Mérida and scoured the book stores. 'It is no more than an old folk tale,' he said to himself of his grandmother's story. Still, he was determined to resolve his curiosity and affirm the notion his dream was a convoluted memory.

He browsed through the anthologies of Mexican and Spanish tales. At one bookstore, the store attendant, a literature student at a local college, assisted him, but neither of them could find anything resembling the grandmother's story.

After giving up his search that evening, Manuel took a flight home to Mexico City. He arrived at his sister's house in the posh suburb called *Colonial Juárez* after midnight. As the taxi pulled up to the house, he saw the figure of a man lingering outside. Upon seeing the taxi, the man began to flee. Manuel and the cab driver jumped out of the car and ran after the intruder, but he seemed to disappear into thin air amid the fluttering of wings.

The cab driver immediately crossed himself. *"Jesús, María, y José!"* said the cab driver, evoking the holy family. "Did you see that, señor? That man became a bird"

"He just outran us," said Manuel moodily as they walked back to the car to get his luggage.

"But what of the bird?" The cab driver was sweating with fear.

"It must have flown out from the park," said Manuel.

The following morning, Manuel found a note crumpled on the pavement outside his sister's house.

> *Querida*, remember that you still have an owner. Until we meet again in. . . .

The note was unfinished. Manuel put it in his pocket and later destroyed it.

25

Imageries of Desires

No one except Silvia Vázquez noticed that María
Elena recovered from her amnesia—by this time
all agreed that that was what had afflicted
her—only after Sebastian himself began to feel better.
One month before Manuel Muñoz called her to give her
the news, Sebastian began to return to his old self.

Silvia first noticed the change one afternoon when
she went up to the garage apartment to bring him some
lunch. Sebastian was neatly dressed, clean-shaven, and
working on some drawings at his desk. His appearance
surprised her. He looked as healthy and as youthful
as he had been before his madness had degraded his
body.

"Thank you, *Mamá* Silvia," he said as she set down
the tray.

"What are you doing, son?" she asked cautiously,
half expecting him to ramble on about sea storms and
malevolent ship spirits.

"Working," he said simply.

The following day, frustrated that her sons Ricardo
and Josesito had not come by to help her with the yard

work, Silvia tried, without success, to start the lawn mower.

"Let me do that, *Mamá*." It was Sebastian, who had watched her through the window and come downstairs, somehow overcoming the obsession that the sun would rot his flesh. He started the lawn mower and cut the grass. After he finished, he cleaned the yard for her and, in the following days, performed other work around the house.

"There is much to be done," he noted to Silvia.

"After your *Papá* José died, your brothers promised to come by and help, but they have their own homes to take care of." She shrugged her resignation. "You know how that goes."

Sebastian spent the following weeks working on the house during the day and resuming his own work at night. One afternoon, Josesito and Ricardo, relieved at Sebastian's recovery, invited him to play a game of pool with them. Silvia took the opportunity of his absence to clean the apartment. She discovered the drawings, pictorial chronicles of his last visit to Mexico: the narrow, cobbled-stone streets from the colonial cities; massive, Baroque churches rising in the countryside like mountains; intimate glimpses of obscure Indian hamlets; portraits of many faces he had encountered. As she looked through the drawings, she came upon one of María Elena. Sebastian had depicted her as a noblewoman in Indian clothing receiving homage from Imperial ambassadors.

In one corner of the room, Silvia noticed a sheet-covered easel. She removed the sheet and saw a watercolor painting. Again it was María Elena. Her naked body was an extension of the mountains and a lagoon filled with colorful fish and amphibians. The sky and clouds seemed to pour into her, as if her body were the nexus of earth and heavens. Silvia threw the sheet over the painting again, finished cleaning the apartment. She said nothing of the drawings and painting to Sebastian.

A few nights later, Silvia Vázquez was awakened by the sound of a closing car door. She turned and looked at the clock on her nightstand. It read, 3:00 A.M. She lay still and continued to listen, knowing full well that it was Sebastian loading things into his car.

Her mind drifted to another time when she was young. She and José were still living in Mexico. It was summer and the boys—Ricardo and Josesito—who were at once bored and agitated by the oppressive heat of Nuevo Leon, had begged their parents to take them to the country, to a vacation home that belonged to José's business partner because the house had a swimming pool. José consented and took the family to the country house. When they arrived, they ran into a young married couple who came by to clean the house and care for the yard and the pool. They approached José and Silvia and introduced themselves. As some people are prone to divulge personal matters to strangers, they told José and Silvia they were two cousins who had fallen in love and married against the wishes of the family. Their families had disowned them, but José's compadre, *Don* Reynaldo, had been kind enough to help them out by giving them work.

"Poor fools," said José after they had left.

Silvia knew from her husband's tone that he felt no pity for them, perhaps even despised them. She, on the other hand, not only felt a mixture of repulsion and compassion, but a strange sensation, one of distant recognition, as if remembering another's memory. Her own paternal great-grandparents had been first cousins. In olden days of the Spanish and Tlaxcalan pioneers in Northern New Spain, there were few people and many times distant cousins—removed by as few as three generations—had married. Silvia had made the discovery about her great-grandparents when, as an adolescent, she discovered some old papers in her parents' shed. The papers were a special dispensation from the Church allowing her great-grandparents to marry.

Silvia continued to listen to Sebastian's movements. An hour or so later, she heard the engine start and the car pull out of the driveway.

"Forgive me, José," she said out loud as if speaking to her dead husband, remembering that he would have wanted her to stop Sebastian from leaving.

26

Absence

María Elena Vázquez disappeared on the day she left Mexico City for Uxmal. It was a Wednesday, eight days before the summer solstice. She came into the archeological lab to pick up some of her things: several notebooks, a laptop computer, a digital camera, and an extra pair of hiking books that her brother Ricardo had sent her three Christmases before.

"I am going to Uxmal," she told her colleagues at the lab.

No one found that pronouncement particularly portentous although Uxmal was the site of her misfortune, the place where her languages were stolen. Everyone merely assumed that she was returning to Uxmal to complete the work she had begun before the earthquake.

After her disappearance, the authorities questioned all of her friends, associates, and even Manuel's friends. When the authorities pressed to learn the nature of her work, no one gave them the specific answers they were seeking. The police, on a tip from some local government officials in the Yucatán and on the report filed by Manuel Muñoz, assumed she had been kidnapped by either rebels or criminals. The archeologists vehemently disputed that theory, but offered nothing in their accounts to dispel those suspicions.

Her colleagues had made various assumptions about her work, regarding it as an independent but vital link to the overall project. They told the police that María Elena had discovered what appeared to be the burial site of a minor Maya nobleman inside the Pyramid of the Magician. For all practical purposes, she had been working alone with her own crew of field assistants who were Maya Indians. Since she fluently communicated with her workers in their Mayan language, the other historians and archeologists knew little of her activities.

The police, attempting to reconstruct past events to find a motive for her disappearance, questioned the park supervisor at Uxmal who told them that on the day before the earthquake, her crew had refused to enter the cave beneath the pyramid. They were waiting for her outside when he happened by and, alarmed at seeing a group of Indians idling, demanded to know why they were not working.

He said, "I went up to the bunch and asked them, 'Where is *Señorita* Vázquez?'

"One of them pointed to the tomb and said, 'She is inside.'

"So I told them, 'Why are you not helping her? Is that not what you are paid to do? Well? Answer me!'"

"The men looked at one another, and finally one responded, 'The earth will shake.'

"Well, you can just imagine how furious I was. I said, 'What? What are you saying? There hasn't been an earthquake in these parts *¡desde el año de la inquisición!* Get in there and help *Señorita* Vázquez.'

"But the men were not persuaded and they just stood there like statues.

"'The earth will shake,' they repeated."

The supervisor then gave the police his interpretation of the events. "*Señorita* Vázquez was enmeshed in the rituals of the Indians. On the eve of the solstice, the Indians have celebrations on the sites of the ruins. I am certain her disappearance is related to some barbaric rite. I am truly afraid she may have been murdered."

But unknown to the police, it was Manuel Muñoz, not the Indians, who had had designs to hurt her. Manuel, upon returning home in the evening and not finding her there, knew immediately that she had not only left Mexico City, but had left him as well. Despite his modern prejudices, he had begun to give credence to superstition. Never before had he experienced so many unexplained events; María Elena's mental illness; the recurrent, grotesque nightmares of pursuit by the sorcerers; the appearance of the lost letters; and finally, the strange, humming sound as if human voices were reduced to the buzzing of insects. Something was going on, and he knew it was related to María Elena's fascination with the mysteries of the Indians. Manuel thought, 'She wanted to find out things they would never tell outsiders. That is why she went and met with the old *curanderos* and *brujos*. What ever it was she was looking for caught up with her.'

Manuel was certain of one other thing. 'She has gone to meet Sebastian,' he thought as he remembered that every crucial memory of María Elena's behavior leading up to her accident had included Sebastian in one way or another. 'He's her accomplice in all of this nonsense. He must be the one she loved before me. No wonder she could not marry him! Her own cousin!'

He got back in his car and drove to the Yucatán. 'You will not betray me so easily, María Elena,' he thought. The buzzing sound, which unknown to him were the echoes of his own thoughts, floated inside the car.

Manuel drove almost continuously, stopping only for fuel, eating in the car. Soon he could see the primeval, low jungle of the Yucatán on the horizon. He entered the jungle filled with his own obsession and ignored the convolutions of times as they swirled about the air like lost fireflies. He, of course, did not see that all who had crossed the Maya land—geography born of the asteriodal dusts—left part of their essence in the spatial corridors. The frustrated and failed ambitions of men— both Mayas and Hispanics—revealed themselves in the abandoned astronomical cities of magic and in the relics of once great haciendas. A greater destiny prevailed in the jungle, for it was here that hundreds of generations before, men first learned to penetrate secrets unseen and immeasurable. Through their ancient visionary arts, they discerned the true fabric of time and space; learned of cycles of death and rebirth, chaos and order. But later they called these forces and phenomenon, "gods", and enslaved themselves to their self-created theologies.

Yet the most ancient of the rituals still preserved the original truths. Only a select few over the centuries, those possessed of extraordinary desire and the ability to learn the language of dreams could participate in these rituals. That person in Manuel's time, as the Indian elders had perceived years before, was none other than María Elena. But, while Manuel had earlier been given to some insights and had made connections between the strange events and María Elena, those were overidden now and he was singularly driven by his obsession to repossess her and by his jealousy and hatred for his rival.

As Manuel drove into the countryside, the voices carried by the night winds began to resonate. Had he listened, he could have discerned the conversations embedded in the humming, but he did not. The voices were saying:

"Meet me in Uxmal on the summer solstice. . . ."

"Quihachouic quib ta xquicacbeh quib tzolbeh bac uholom caminac. . . ."

"I will take you to *la tierra de iras y no volveras. . . ."*

"In ic niquimanatiuh / tlalli inepantla / n ic nauhcampa. . . ."

"I dreamt of Malintzín and she was a slave who. . . ."

"My grandfather's coyote spirit shall protect you, *amor. . . ."*

The winds were gradually dying, yet the humming sound became louder and louder. Then, suddenly, the noise ceased. A premonitory sensation surged through his body. He could feel it. María Elena had been reunited with her lover and cousin Sebastian. 'Just for a short while,' he thought, 'until I find you.'

He thought the people of the villages would tell him of her whereabouts, but he had not anticipated that their collective love for the woman of many languages would conspire to conceal her from him, for they already sensed danger nearby. Centuries of cruelty had taught them the skills of intuitive survival.

The morning after he arrived in the Yucatán, Manuel went directly to the archeological site in Uxmal. None of the historians and archeologists had seen her. He questioned the Indian workers. They did not want to tell him they had, indeed, seen her, but they were afraid of outright lying. They knew a man like Manuel could easily avenge himself by paying some corrupt policeman to make trouble. So they responded with the ambiguous remark, "She is not from here."

He quickly deciphered their cryptic statement and went to look for her in the towns between Uxmal and Mérida: Homún, Maxcanú, Opichén, Umán. As he searched the plazas and *mercados,* Manuel consciously noticed the people of these *pueblos* and saw them for the first time as beings with private longings, sorrows, and distinct faces. For him, these were disturbing thoughts. He tried to exile them from his mind, but could not. Instead, he found himself imagining what it must be like to be a prisoner of skin and tongue, to be one of the despised Indians.

These thoughts, suffocating him like heat, at first

deceived him into thinking he would find María Elena dressed as a modern woman. But he quickly corrected that error, remembering that whenever she went out of the city and mingled in the towns, she preferred to wear skirts and *huipils* in the manner of the local Indian women.

He remembered the first time he had seen her like that, somehow utterly transformed, as if she had obliterated her modern self. Even the manner in which she carried her body was strange to him. He now knew that to find her he would have to look into the face of every young woman. He mistakenly thought that her green eyes would bear her out, but instead he found many young women with her sea-green eyes that recalled the centuries of fornication of the Iberian priests, soldiers, and landowners, some of whom had descended from the blood of José María Vázquez and his sons.

Finding his fiancée replicated in the many women of the *pueblos* did not discourage Manuel's quest. If anything, he became more obsessed by her. As the wind blew, it robbed him of his thoughts. 'I shall find her.'

A choir of voices responded:

"Let her go. Malintzín belongs to us."

Bedeviled by obsession and jealousy, he did not hear the voices carried by the winds.

27

Solstice

After the sun had finally surrendered its dominion of hours on the summer solstice, an empty solitude descended upon Mexico City like the neglect of the unloved. Strangely, at night, the Cathedral seemed more like a memorial of stone whose impatient dead struggle to recover their voices. Having been gone for several weeks, the voices of the night currents returned to the Cathedral on this, the shortest night of the year. Those who had mastered the secret language of dreams could hear the cries escaping from the prison of forgotten time, wails out of context, fragments of incomplete conversations.

The old priest, Father Fernando, wandered through the Cathedral after supper. The voices of the dead and the wind currents followed him, some reciting their frustrated prayers; while others repeated their centuries old confessions, still seeking absolution from the confines of their consciences. He listened, and as one speaker's words faded, another's emerged:

"Father, I have sinned. . . ."

"Father, I gave up my body to the *patrón* so that

my child would have light skin. . . ."

"I killed my woman, Father, because she betrayed me with another man. In my rage I tore her body to pieces and found a child inside of her, may God forgive me!"

"Help us in our hour of need. . . ."

"Let Cuauhtémoc be re-born. . . ."

"Let my many tongues create a new race of people. . . ."

"I went with the *patrón* and helped him murder his compadre and his family. We ate their food while their bodies bled. . . ."

"We buried him by *la casa de los pastores*. I cannot forget his face because his eyes refused to close. . . ."

"Father, why is it wrong to be in love with my cousin? . . ."

"Return to us, Martín Cortés, the first of your race. . . ."

"Beloved, I remember the taste of your skin. . . ."

"He caused a madness in my blood, Father, that is why I forgot myself and relinquished my honor. . . ."

"What you call sin, Father, should be called love. . . ."

"Our Father in heaven, your soldiers on earth, in the name of the holy cross, burn the heathen's feet. We pray that he surrender the gold that will fill the coffers of the mother church. . . ."

"We took their lands by deception. We told them we would petition the governor on their behalf, but we changed the land deeds into our names. The *cacique* condemned me to dream every night that the earth swallows my children. . . ."

"Against the wishes of my father and mother, I love a woman who bears my green-eyed children. . . ."

"Father, I saw the Captain-general strangle his wife . . . ."

"Father, the sisters and I took her mixed blood child and killed it the moment it was born. We buried him in the walls of the convent. . . ."

The old priest murmured, "You are forgiven, you are forgiven."

As soon as he said this, Father Fernando felt the space within the Cathedral shift, as when one enters a new dream in the illogic of sleep. The Cathedral emptied itself of the voices and all that remained was the sound of breathing, that of himself and another. He followed the hum of the other's breathing until it led him to a side altar where La Nahua prayed silently. He entered into her thoughts and heard them as clearly as he had previously heard the night echoes of the dead.

"Return once more, Martín Cortés, first of your race. We, the blood of your mother, beseech your protection, *su merced*. Use your *brujo's* magic to protect the eagle's flight to *la tierra de iras y no volveras*. We elect you the high priest of two bloods. Use the wisdom you learned from your sleep in your mother's womb and escape the fires of purgatory. There is no sin, Martín, only love. . . ."

La Nahua, in the fever of her prayers, collapsed on the floor in front of the altar.

"*Señora! Señora!*" said Father Fernando as he helped the old woman onto a bench. "Are you all right?"

"Ay, *Padrecito! Padrecito!* Pray for justice. For the love of God and all things!"

"Calm yourself, *Señora*," he said. He took out his handkerchief, and, in an undeliberate act of sacrilege, soaked it in a basin of holy water and wiped the face of the old woman.

"Thank you, *Padre*," said La Nahua. "You are a good man, a forgiving man."

"Let me call for some help," he said.

"No, *Padre*, that is not necessary. I will go now even though Death waits for me in the streets. I shall finally rest after 124 years, *Padre*. I have lived enough to see the shores of another land through an eagle's eyes."

La Nahua got up to leave. The priest showed her out and watched her dissolve in the liquidity of the night. He knew that her presence was connected to the events he had heard in the winds and witnessed in his dreams. When he retired from his evening in the Cathedral, he welcomed his insomnia, and prepared to listen for the resolution of the nocturnal mysteries. He lit a kerosene lamp and turned off the electric lights. He opened the window and said, "*Vengan, voces desdichadas.*"

A wind blew in from the south bringing the voices of the dispossessed he had just invited. He closed his eyes and listened to the fragments of conversations crowding into his ears.

"The *licenciado* found her in town and followed her. . . ."

"We had already closed the park. We thought that all of the celebrants had left and gone home. Just as we were getting ready to leave, the *licenciado* came to the gate and asked if he could go through the park. We thought he just wanted to take a short cut back to the hotel, so we paid no attention to him. We went back inside, too, because we were real thirsty and thought no one would see us if we stole a few beers. That's how we saw. . . ."

"*Mamá*, I could not believe my own ears! The *licenciado* lied to the police about the weapon, and he lied about the men, too. They were not rebels, I tell you! They must have been ghosts because they came out of nowhere like smoke. When the *licenciado* found her, she was alone. He began to call her some bad names, and tried to grab her. She pulled away from him and said something strange, like, 'My freedom for your life.' The *licenciado* got very angry. He told her, 'What are you talking about? Are you still crazy?' The woman said to him, 'The curse of Martín Cortés was for your people. You are the blood of Muñoz Carrillo. Did you not see the two phantoms—a soldier and his dog—coming for you? Surely you must have heard the voices in the wind calling your name!' He got very pale when she said that, as if he understood what she meant. But then he said to her, 'All I know is that you are coming back with me.' She said, "No, Manuel. I am betraying you.

That is a better revenge than death. . . . Why pretend you do not understand?' For a while, they said nothing to each other, but we could see the *licenciado* was enraged. Then she said to him, 'Why do I waste my breath explaining this to you? You will never understand. Go back to your *sociedad*.' She started to walk away when he grabbed her and would not let her go. When she broke free, he took out the gun and shot her. . . ."

"A strange eagle flew around the ruins during the celebration. . . ."

"Let me die in Martín's tomb, Cuauhtémoc. . . ."

"When the police got there, a black dog was running wildly through the park, as though he had gotten lost or left behind. 'He must be rabid,' they said, and cowards that they are, they shot the dog as he was running up a pyramid. The dog's body came tumbling down. We all ran to find the dog's body, but all we found was a mass of butterflies on the stones. . . ."

" . . . that is when the men appeared and attacked the *licenciado*. We ran back inside the store to call the police and, like magic, the woman was inside with a companion, a man with marks painted on his back and arms. He was saying something in a strange language. The woman told us not to call the police, that she would live, and showed us how the bullet had entered and left the side of her body, missing her vital organs. She told us the man was her cousin and that he loved her. 'We will help you escape,' we told her because we could tell they were being hunted down and felt sorry for them. The woman began to say something like 'take me to the tomb.' The man picked her up and carried her outside. The ghosts appeared again and we followed them to a remote ruin and they all went inside a chamber. *Mamá*, I swear on the Holy Virgin, while we were watching them enter the chamber they all disappeared into thin air. Only their voices floated around like bees. We could not understand what they were saying because they all spoke at the same time. That is what I saw. May God condemn me forever if I am lying! . . ."

Father Fernando took out the manuscript he had been writing for Lupe Huerta and recorded the last of the wind narratives. He ended the journal with a post script.

My beloved niece,

At midnight I will perform a special mass for the safety and well-being of Malintzín and Cuauhtémoc, who have returned to this ancient land after hundreds of years of exile. They have penetrated the barriers that separates our world from *la tierra de iras y no volveras*. What does that mean? Not to return? Is it that they have died? Or, perhaps, that they will no longer be part of our world and its false realities, that they have found a new way and an old way, that they have become the high priests of the secret rituals that keeps chaos from devouring us. God help us! Things are never as we thought them to be. All of our truths are mere metaphors.

The only truth is that of dreams.

Sincerely, your uncle who loves you,

Fr. Fernando Ocampo

28

Farewell

The day following the summer solstice, Fernando Ocampo went to visit his niece Lupita Huerta. The night before, after he had finished recording the narratives of the wind, the voices went completely silent. Not even the whispers of the persistent and omnipresent ghosts that usually haunted the Cathedral could be heard. It was as if the constellations had rearranged their order in the skies of a foreign universe, invisible to the present existence but still sensed in the geometric intuitions of the planets.

Lupe was pleased to see her great-uncle, yet his appearance alarmed her. Black rings circled his eyes; his skin and the whites of his eyes were jaundiced, as if he had suddenly contracted a liver disease. When she offered him a cup of coffee, he refused. He just wanted to talk, and he did so for hours: about his youth and his brother Juan; his years in the seminar and his first encounter with the voices of the night winds; and finally of his solitude.

"The problem with love," he told her, "is the feeling of absence. How I wish we had the closeness that your grandfather and I had in the *pueblo*. There, people stayed together and died in the land of their birth. Today, everyone moves around so much. We are so far from our families and our beloved friends. This kind of solitude is worse than death."

Then he fell silent, gazing pensively off into space. He had come this time to deliver to Lupe his manuscript of the night winds. But he did not give it to her immediately. His silence prompted Lupe to ask if he was ill.

"No," he said, "I am not sick, Lupita."

Again he went silent. For the lack of knowing what to say next, Lupe turned on the television. As usual, she had the channel set on a news station. The impersonal, mechanical voice of the female reporter narrated the events from Mérida, Yucatán.

". . . the army has been called in to investigate the alleged movement of Zapatista rebels into the Yucatán region. We have an unconfirmed report that the rebels have kidnapped an American archeologist from the State University of Pennsylvania. So far, the authorities have not received any communiqués or ransom demands.

"No charges will be filed against *licenciado* Muñoz, as the police have determined he fired his weapon in self-defense."

The anchorman cut in, "Isn't it unusual, however, for a civilian to be armed in a park? Did *Señor* Muñoz offer an explanation?"

The news reporter responded, "In his statement to the police, *Señor* Muñoz said he had heard of numerous highway assaults by robbers and decided to take precautions. He forgot to remove his weapon from his person when he entered the park."

The anchor concluded the report by saying, "And fortunately so. Because of increased lawlessness, so many of our citizens are taking measures for their self-defense. Thank you Vera. We'll cut away for a commercial break and return with today's sports in two minutes."

"It did not happen like that," said Father Fernando. He then gave Lupe Huerta the manuscript and told her he was tired.

"Go lie down in my room for a while, uncle," said Lupita, who was saddened by a premonition that Fernando Ocampo was dying.

Three days later, he died in his sleep.

29

The Police Report

July 19th

Police Report to His Excellency,
Attorney General of the State Of Yucatán

Dear Excellency:

We have concluded our investigation on the disappearance of *Srta*. María Elena Vázquez, whose profession is listed as archeologist with the State University of Pennsylvania, USA, and her adopted brother,
Sebastian Vázquez Joaquín, free-lance illustrator, last
residing in the city of San José, California, USA.
Their disappearance was brought to our attention by
Srta. Vázquez's fiancé, *licenciado* Manuel Muñoz, a
corporate attorney residing in Mexico City.

We have dismissed the possibility of kidnapping
by Zapatista rebels, aided by *Sr*. Sebastian Vázquez,
whom *Sr*. Muñoz alleges was a political sympathizer
of indigenous rights organizations. Our investigation,
as well as interviews with *Srta*. Vazquez's associates

and family have conclusively shown that the said disappeared persons were willingly in each other's company for intensely personal and private reasons.

I have uncovered some information, although unsubstantiated by representatives of the State University of Pennsylvania who have cited the confidentiality of their personnel files, that María Elena Vázquez had requested a transfer to Belize. Thus, I must conclude that there are no political motives behind her 'disappearance.' The same must be said for *Sr.* Sebastian Vázquez, whose interest in the indigenous peoples is strictly cultural. His sister, *Sra.* Rachel Vázquez Peña, informed me that her brother had no political agenda.

With regards to the eyewitness accounts that *Sr.* Muñoz fired his gun and shot *Srta.* Vázquez, those claims, too, cannot be substantiated. There was absolutely no forensic evidence of an injury, i.e., there was no blood found anywhere, let alone that of *Srta.* Vázquez. Upon further questioning, the eyewitnesses admitted they had returned to the park store to steal beer. The park supervisor informed me of past drinking problems with said witnesses.

I have, nonetheless, included what I consider the key interviews with the local witnesses who were in the disappeared persons' company a few days before June 21st. (See Exhibits A & B below.) As for the other interviews, they reveal very little concerning the disappeared persons and are replete with impertinent information about pagan rituals in which the indigenous population still engages. Although the interviews I include in this report are also filled with superstitious reference, they do reveal the personal nature of the disappeared persons' relationship.

As far as we can determine, the disappeared persons are presently residing either in Guatemala or Belize. At the request of *Sra*. Rachel Vázquez Peña, I have denied the press access to the contents of these interviews in light of the sensitive nature of the relationship between the disappeared persons. I am certain that your excellency will conclude, as I have, that public knowledge of this affair will serve no other purposes than to defame the reputation of the Vázquez Family and possibly create a negative perception about our fine state which could adversely affect our tourism industry.

We would greatly appreciate it if your excellency's office could be so gracious as to inform *Sr*. Muñoz of our findings.

Respectfully yours,

Capt. Raul Álcala de la Torre
Chief Investigator, Mérida Police Dept.

EXHIBIT A
June 23rd

Transcript of police interview with Tanilo Tun, archeological field assistant to María Elena Vázquez.

CAPT. ÁLCALA DE LA TORRE: Please state for the record how long you have known María Elena Vázquez.

TANILO TUN: Several years—I lose track of time. Let

me think, Captain. I have been her assistant for over two years, and she had first visited us two years before that when she was still a student. So, I'd say a little more than four years.

CAPT. ÁLCALA DE LA TORRE: Relate to us how you befriended *Srta.* Vázquez.

TANILO TUN: As I said, when she was a student, she came one summer with a professor whom we knew and worked for before. The professor had just finished doing some work in Chiapas and stopped by to talk to some of our elders.

After a few days she asked me if someone—one of us—could teach her our dialect. She enjoyed learning languages and said she already knew several, including a dialect of Mayan. My wife got to know her and liked her very much, so she asked María Elena to stay with us while the professor remained in the area.

CAPT. ÁLCALA DE LA TORRE: Excuse me, *Señor* Tun, did you say she lived with you and your family?

TANILO TUN: Yes, Captain. She came to my house because she said she wanted to see it. She showed me some papers she had gotten from the government office in Mérida that said that her ancestor's nephew had built my house. My family worked on these lands when they were part of the Hacienda Vázquez before the revolution. I got my house from my father-in-law who was a *cacique*. A general gave him the house because he fought with Zapata.

When she came to the house, she met my wife.

That is when we asked her to stay with us. She was an excellent student and learned to speak our dialect very quickly. My wife says that there are people who can learn a language by breathing your air while you sleep.

CAPT. ÁLCALA DE LA TORRE: So *Srta.* Vázquez befriended you specifically because she was interested in researching her family's history.

TANILO TUN: No, *Señor* . . . well, yes, so to speak. She said she was searching for a ghost her ancestor knew. We had seen him before, the spirit of a soldier and a black dog. She said the spirit was Martín Cortés, and he was the one who showed her the passage to the other land.

CAPT. ÁLCALA DE LA TORRE: I see. Someone named Martín Cortés escorted *Srta.* and *Sr.* Vázquez to Belize. Correct?

TANILO TUN: As you say, Captain. Martín Cortés came for them.

EXHIBIT B
June 24th

The following is a transcript of the police interview with *Sra.* Elsie Tun, wife of Tanilo Tun.

CAPT. ÁLCALA DE LA TORRE: Please tells us anything that you remember about *Srta.* Vázquez. Go on, do not be afraid. You are not in any trouble. Just speak your mind.

ELSIE TUN: Well, Captain, it wasn't just me who liked her very much. All of the people in our *pueblo* and the workers at the pyramids liked her and respected her very much. She was very intelligent and serious, but we women loved her because when we saw her we felt as though we were still dreaming and she was part of that dream. María Elena was never conceited or superior towards anyone even though she was educated. There were many times after she came back from working with the professor that she tried to help us with our work. We never let her help us because the elders had told us that she had the blood of the Indian kings, and we all felt as if there was something very special about her. She was like the desires that we all feel but hide from the world. She talked very little about herself at first, so she was very mysterious to us. She didn't tell us anything about her family or her home in California. After she learned our language, she began to open up, so one day when she walked with me to the market I asked her if she had a boyfriend. And let me tell you, Captain, that the young men of our town respected her, too, and never approached her about love.

CAPT. ÁLCALA DE LA TORRE: How did *Srta.* Vázquez respond to your question about her boyfriend?

ELSIE TUN: Well, Captain, she told me she didn't have a boyfriend, but that she had been in love with someone since she was fifteen. I asked her, "Is he married to someone else?" She said, no, that she was in love with her mother's first cousin. He had been raised as her brother so her family would never allow them to marry. It was very sad to see, Captain, because she was a woman who was loved only in her dreams. "Won't you find someone else?" I asked her. She didn't answer me, so I never asked her about that again.

Months later, she came back to the *pueblo* with a man she said was her mother's cousin. He had eyes that were like the blue of a faraway ocean, so we called him The Mariner. We could tell he was the same cousin she was in love with, so Tanilo and I let them stay at our house as though they were man and wife. We felt so sorry for them, and told them to stay in our *pueblo*, that we would never condemn them for what they were. But they had not come to hide from their family. You could tell from the beginning. There was an obsession they shared. The elders knew that the moment they set eyes on The Mariner. Some of them were afraid of him because they said he could change himself into an eagle and summon the dead from their graves. After he came, the spirit of the black dog was seen everywhere, calling them to follow him. The elders were afraid for María Elena. They said, "Do not follow the soldier's dog, daughter. He is after your unborn child." But she did not seem to hear them. She told me, "Elsie, I have been waiting for this moment. Sebastian has found the way to call Martín Cortés." Captain, they could have stayed with us and been free to love each other, but instead, they went away and followed the dog's spirit.

Then María Elena was gone for a long time.

When she came back to work at the ruins at Uxmal,
she was in a terrible kind of solitude that we could
not break through. She had lost her beloved to madness and the child she had been carrying had died before it was through forming. She seemed to have lost
her desire for everything except her work, so you can
imagine how surprised we were when *Sr.* Muñoz
showed up one day asking for her, telling us he was
her fiancé. Nothing made us sadder, because he had
the hardened look of a boss. He would come and take
her away to Mérida or Mexico City for days, and
when she returned, she seemed more alone than ever.

One morning, while it was still dark, a dream led
me out of my sleep. I went outside and I found María
Elena weeping by the well. "Why are you crying?" I
asked her. She told me she was only pretending to
love *Sr.* Muñoz, that she really loved her cousin.
"Why don't you go back to him if you love him?" I
asked her. That was when she told me how he had
gone insane because the spirit of Martín Cortés had
captured him. I wanted to know, Captain, why she
had chosen *Sr.* Muñoz to replace her beloved, and she
told me that it was because she had lost all hope. She
just wanted to find someone—anyone—who would
occupy that emptiness in her heart. She was not being cruel to the *licenciado*. She really tried to love
him, but she just could not forget Sebastian.

CAPT. ÁLCALA DE LA TORRE: What can you tell us about
licenciado Muñoz? How did he act?

ELSIE TUN: As I said before, Captain, the *licenciado*

was like a boss. Very superior. He was never friendly towards us, and you could tell he did not like our town because he never slept here. He would not even eat with us when we invited him. The worst part was his jealousy. He would follow María Elena around, and once he hired a policeman to spy on her. But as I said before, she only loved her cousin, and he was not here. *Sr.* Muñoz wanted to take her away forever and change her into something she could never be. We all prayed to the holy mother that her cousin come back for her, so you see it was God's will that they be reunited. Everything was God's design, even her language madness. You see, she was able to learn the language of the dead. Later, after she got well, she wrote me a letter that had messages from our dead ones. My mother sent me a message about some money she had buried and forgotten about while she was alive. My husband and I were able to buy a new van with the money. All of our neighbors in town heard from their dead through María Elena, and we were happy to hear that their new homes are very much like the world they left except they can travel without cars and that time makes no sense.

CAPT. ÁLCALA DE LA TORREE: Yes, yes. Can you tell me something about the days before *Srta.* and *Sr.* Vázquez disappeared?

ELSIE TUN: She returned from Mexico City about seven or eight days before she left forever. She told me that she was leaving *Sr.* Muñoz. We thought she meant she was breaking off her engagement, but she meant she was leaving altogether. How could we know? Sometimes the way we say things does not mean what we want to say, and other times it does. But nothing unusual was happening until he arrived three days later. . . .

Capt. Álcala de la Torre: Who? *Sr.* Muñoz?

Elsie Tun: No, the mariner man, Sebastian. The children were startled when they first saw him because he had his face painted like the Indian dancers. Even Tanilo and I were not certain he was not one of the recently dead who had lost his way. But no, he was very much alive. María Elena recognized him right away and ran into his arms. They spoke to each other in a language that only they understood. Tanilo said it was another Indian language that is spoken in a large desert to the north. We let them stay in our house so they could release their repressed love. But it was very strange, Captain, because Sebastian never took the paint off his face. But we got used to it, even the children.

Capt. Álcala de la Torre: How long did they stay?

Elsie Tun: They stayed until one day before they disappeared. For the most part they were inseparable, and their presence filled the *pueblo* with a strange happiness, like the memory of a new beginning. The day before they left us, I said to Sebastian, "We will miss you if you leave us. I wish you could stay with us forever." And he said to me, "We shall always be with you."

We did not understand what he meant by that, but one of our elders told us to always be prepared for their return.

The night after the solstice, Tanilo and I prepared the room for them—clean sheet, fresh water, and even flowers to perfume the air. That very night we saw them as we did every night, returning to our house from a walk in the plaza. Every morning thereafter, the room is empty, but it is filled with the warmth of bodies and the smell of love.

CAPT. ÁLCALA DE LA TORRE: So they are still in Mexico?

ELSIE TUN: No, they have gone to the other land. Their spirits come from the future to visit us.

CAPT. ÁLCALA DE LA TORRE: Are they dead?

ELSIE TUN: Not dead, Captain. They are in the other land, *la tierra de iras y no volveras*. In that land, time moves slower than it does here. Besides, they can escape death and stay young forever because her cousin-husband becomes the eagle who rises on the morning of the winter solstice and the eagle who falls on the summer solstice. He owns the secrets of time. He has taken her away to love her, and the rains of the distant planets depend on their love. That is all I know, Captain.

POSTSCRIPT TO REPORT:

Excellency, my sources in Guatemala tell me there have been rumors and "sightings" of *Srta.* & *Sr.* Vázquez. All of these rumors are associated with various indigenous religious practices. According to individuals questioned by the authorities, the afore-mentioned persons reportedly can appear and vanish into thin air. I have received, moreover, a fax from my counterpart in Tlaxcala stating that María Elena Vázquez and Sebastian Vázquez have been involved in some of the local religious ceremonies of the Indians. Some accounts have placed them in several villages simultaneously.

We must conclude, however, that these reports are a by-product of some kind of fanatical hysteria. Based on what little rational and hard data we have, we must unequivocally conclude that the missing persons are currently residing in Belize or, possibly, Guatemala.

The Vázquez family accepts the veracity of our report, namely that the disappeared persons are now in Belize or Guatemala. They confirm that both María Elena Vázquez and Sebastian Vázquez Joaquín were deeply involved in indigenous practices, which helps explain the superstitious contents of the aforementioned interviews. The Vázquez family has requested that the authorities not interfere with its family members as they are breaking no laws and causing no offense to anyone other than to those who possess rigid religious sensibilities. We conclude that this is the best course of action. I have communicated this request to the authorities in Belize and Guatemala.

Respectfully,

Raul Álcala de la Torre
Chief Investigator, Mérida Police Dept.

30

The Center of Many Times

As the flight from Mérida approached Mexico City, Rachel Vázquez watched the urban sprawl unfold beneath the airplane. The solitude of the ancient plateau had suddenly given way to a city that was once only imagined in prophetic dreams. During a hallucinating mental pause, she imagined she saw the untouched Tenochtitlán exactly as Cortés and her ancestor Armando Vázquez had seen it: a jewel of colors and gold floating on a lake, its rising structures of stone feathered with smoke.

When her mind refocused back to the present, she saw a city that seemed hastily assembled on top of another, as though time itself were urgently trying to defeat its own passage.

On her way to her hotel, she observed the streets and buildings and even the rhythms of the people. There were moments when she saw remnants of the past imposing themselves on each other, all refusing to leave, to be forgotten. The city seemed to her a collection of unmoved time.

She had decided to stay in Mexico City for a few

days. Her business in the Yucatán was finished sooner than expected, and she now had the luxury of solitude. She had decided to visit all of the places in Mexico City where she imagined María Elena going, perhaps, hoping her daughter would magically reappear or, perhaps, hoping to find her stuck in a fragment of accumulated time.

And if she did reappear, what would Rachel say? She had come prepared to say, "Forgive me, *hija*, for staining you with my sins. I do not regret the love that brought you into the world, but I do regret denying you my love." She wanted to say that and more, but she especially wanted to say the word *"hija,"* as if a word could reclaim her flesh. Rachel remembered how not long ago she found herself looking at María Elena, marveling at the duplication of herself in the young woman. But she saw more. She saw the incarnation of her own hidden desires. In María Elena's movements was a genius of the flesh, as it was with her boxer father, a fluid, unconscious elegance, an utter lack of shame, a body which could commit all sins because it did not recognize sin.

When María Elena became a young woman, she went from being a synthesis of two people to a separate being, as if she were the materialization of the enigma of forgotten desires, a woman in whom all women saw themselves as if she were the collector of unspoken feminine memories. Despite her repressed love for her child, Rachel maintained the code of silence she had sworn to her own father. Later, María Elena, without words, would enter into their pact of silence, giving them another bond besides blood.

Rachel Vázquez rented a hotel room that overlooked the *Zócalo* in Mexico City where the ancient Aztec pyramid emerged from the ground, intruding into the Hispanic facade much as the blood of the Indians reappears in the features of the Mexicans, who despite their Spanish names and traditions, forever remain hidden Indians. She went and visited the National Palace, and as she observed the Diego Rivera mural of the conquest, she caught the eyes of Martín Cortés as he peered out innocently while strapped to his mother's back. His astonished expression heightened the pathos of his destiny because his parents never imagined the contradictions of his divided identity. Even she, Rachel Vázquez, had not imagined what her child would be like when she loved a man whose Indian blood was as ancient as the solitary volcanoes. She took to thinking of her Maria Elena and Martín Cortés simultaneously, for her intuitive daydreams led her to realize that their destinies were, indeed, interlinked. Their names and blood gave them a birthright to their Hispanic world, its language, its customs, and its attitudes. But the darkness of their skin and the emergence of the Indian bones through their skin recalled the illicit union of their origins. Even the best intentions of the fathers could never erase the night floods of their Indian visions. Just as Cortés had Martín legitimized in Rome, her own father had adopted her daughter, given her his name. But what law of man can silence this homeland of the Siberian nomads when it calls to reclaim her children? The old rhythms of antiquity prevail in this land above all things. Voices that were silenced by the violence of men continue to circle about in the invisible currents of air.

Rachel's wanderings through Mexico City led her to rediscover the movements of her own hidden memories. It was then that she remembered her one and only meeting with Pedro Eloy Joaquín, whom his people called "the sorcerer of flight." She had relegated the events of that year to the exile of forgetfulness. That was the painful year in which she met Ramiro Huerta. Her family had gone to Mexico for its annual visit to see her mother's family and so her father could confer with his business partners in Monterrey. Out of boredom, she accepted Sebastian's invitation to go with him and visit his maternal grandfather Pedro. Between Eagle Pass, Texas, and Monterrey, Nuevo Leon, there is a great multitude of small *pueblos* built by the original Spanish and Tlaxcatecan Indians settlers, and between these *pueblos* are the even smaller, embryonic hamlets, the beginnings of some dream that never took hold. Near the town of Montemorelos was such a hamlet, whose name she never bothered to remember, where Pedro Eloy Joaquín lived. She and Sebastian drove to the hamlet from Monterrey, and, if she ever had to, she could only find that place again in the peripheries of nostalgia.

Throughout her adult life, her sporadic remembrance of those desert hamlets was something Rachel Vázquez treasured in her prison of silence, for she felt a kinship with the defeated. She understood this defeat, the dispossession of the desert and its Indian memories after her own disgraceful fall, as if the humiliations of the centuries witnessed by the forlorn desert was the same as that of a woman betrayed by a lover.

Pedro Eloy Joaquín had warned her only months before she met Ramiro Huerta. "You are a beautiful woman and therefore you will feel the avarice and envy of men. Your mariner's eyes remind me of my dead wife. When she died, I wanted to join her in the pits of death to be near her beauty. But I could not die because I was a young man and my legs resisted the power of the earth. Perhaps if I had not been so strong, the earth would not have been angry with me and taken my daughter after Sebastian was born. Now, my legs grow weaker, but the power of the earth remains the same. Soon I shall join the dead, and only Sebastian will be left of the blood of the Joaquíns."

This memory of Pedro Eloy Joaquín was what Rachel Vázquez carried with her when she took a cab to the ruins of Teotihuacán, the ancient city that her own daughter had appropriated as a symbol of her own lost identity. The old city, its people devoured by the erosions of time, had retained its power to reclaim the outcasts of blood and traditions.

She observed the landscape between Mexico City and Teotihuacán and was astonished by its familiarity. As a child, she was always disappointed that her parents took her only to Coahuila and Nuevo Leon. She had always wanted to see the 'real' Mexico, the heartland of the great Meso-American civilizations, imagining a radically different sensibility from her mother's northern homeland. Once in Mexico City, she found that instead of a desired foreignness there was the element of sameness, a manner and movement of people and architecture that was just like her mother's desert *pueblo*, as though these congregations of people were part of a larger organism. It seemed to Rachel Vázquez that the living were mere keepers of a place; that it was geography itself that was the reality and people a mere, momentary illusion of the curvatures of space.

When she saw the Pyramid of the Sun, she was seized by the same wonder that Armando the Mariner had experienced four centuries earlier. She entered the archeological park and found herself divided between two times. In one reality she saw the evidence of a mechanical world; in another, she saw the stone metropolis of swept streets and colorfully painted buildings, the air penetrated by music composed by birds in the imaginations of men. She listened to the languages spoken in the park: Spanish, French, English, German, Italian, and Nahuatl. Above this chaos of languages, she heard, hidden in the molecular rush of the wind, the echoes of the dead, the flutes of children sounding through the layers of the ages, as if time were a geographic entity that was within the reach of a journey. She found a place sequestered from the crowds so she could preserve this magical intrusion. She closed her eyes and allowed the sensation of the past to enter through her ears: conversations spoken in a semantic puzzle, yet familiar in their tone, their emotional inflections. She heard the music of distant celebrations, the cries of bereavement, the chants of rituals forgotten by history, the whispers of lovers, the poisons of betrayals. She heard an entire universe exiled to the movements of the wind, The blood of the conquerors, she found herself conquered by a hallucination of a feathered serpent.

Night was falling and she, oblivious, continued to listen to the music of time, to the voices carried by the secret frequencies of the wind. Suddenly, one voice clarified above the others, a young, feminine, and familiar voice.

> *"In ahmo oyaca Chiucnauah Mictlan.* . . . Rachel, I'll wait for you at the edge of your dreams and show you the pathway to *la tierra de iras y no volveras.* . . ."

"Señora?" a hand gently grasped her shoulder.

Rachel turned and met the sea-green eyes of a young woman, a park attendant, whose Indian bones testified to the contradictions of her blood.

"Señora," repeated the young stranger. "We are closing the park now. You may return tomorrow."

"Yes, of course," said Rachel. "I lost track of time. I am sorry to have inconvenienced you."

"No need to apologize," said the young stranger as she walked Rachel back to the exit. "We all lose our sense of time here. This place, it seems, eats time."

Rachel smiled and said, "You sound like my daughter. She says the same thing is true of all of the Indian ruins."

When they reached the park exit, the stranger said, *"Señora,* I've already inquired with one of the tour bus drivers. He can give you a ride back to the city."

"That's all right, *Señorita,"* said Rachel. "I've had a taxi waiting for me the whole time."

The young woman turned and saw a taxi driver smugly leaning on his car. The young woman rebelled at what she considered an affront to good taste and manners. "That is not necessary, *Señora*. You're under no obligation to him, and what's more, he's likely to charge you half your savings. I can report him to the Department of Tourism—"

"No, it's not a problem," said Rachel gently, surprised by the stranger's protectiveness. "I've been saving for this trip all of my adult life."

"Very well," said the stranger. "Please understand that we do not like it when our guests are taken advantage of by the unscrupulous. It looks bad for our country and our people. . . ." She lost her thoughts mid-sentence because she unwittingly found herself trying to divine Rachel's identity. She asked, "Are you Spanish, *Señora?*"

"My father is Spanish, but my mother is Mexican, from Coahuila, in fact."

"So then?" The stranger's voice had a nostalgic familiarity, a misplaced intimacy.

"I was born on this American soil. I have always considered myself a Mexican. I must go, now, *Señorita*. I thank you."

"At your service, *Señora*."

That evening, Rachel sat on a balcony overlooking the sleeping *Zócalo*, the ancient center of a buried city. She had heard from the descendants of the Nahua Indians of her mother's village that before the summer storms on the great plateau, the winds—pregnant with secret voices—bring the scents of the distant lands, the restful odor of cool rocks. She waited for the winds. But for the time being, the winds were silent, bringing only the faraway scents of the ocean.

31

Divided from Herself

Rachel Vázquez confessed to her children and her husband, once and for all. She gathered them one Sunday afternoon, when they least expected a serious proclamation because Sundays never seemed like the time of the week when anything important happened. She told them of the secret event twenty-six years before, when she gave birth to her illegitimate daughter, María Elena. Rachel had expected her children to be outraged or at the very least shocked. Instead, they met her confession with tears and a misplaced contrition.

"You should have told us she was our sister," they said, weeping. They wanted to know her whereabouts so they could contact her and somehow right the emptiness, rejection, and solitude she had experienced.

But Rachel refused to give in to their demands, not even confiding in Roberto, who met the confession with stupefied amazement.

"Just leave her alone," said Rachel. "She has Sebastian. He has always loved her."

Instead of the relief she sought from her confession,

Rachel Vázquez was instead overwhelmed with melancholy and inconsolable grief.

Upon returning from Mexico City, Rachel's memories of María Elena had become increasingly vivid. Whenever she thought of María Elena, she could almost feel her breathing, see her mystic's green eyes, and hear the sad intonations of her singer's voice. Almost every night, Rachel dreamed that María Elena was a woman from another time, living by a serene lake populated by strange fish and reptiles.

But after she confessed María Elena's true identity to her children and husband, Rachel, as if cursed because she no longer possessed the secret, could no longer conjure María Elena with the same intense vividness, remembering her instead in the shades of faded colors or the foggy grays of half-forgotten dreams. Her longing prompted her to leave messages with the State University of Pennsylvania, but no response ever came. She began to believe the most morbid speculations were true: perhaps María Elena and Sebastian, obsessed with the rituals of antiquity had subjected themselves to some diabolical scenario where they met their deaths. She had heard of such things, how in Matemoros an American student was killed in a sacrificial ritual by a fringe cult.

Finally, when Rachel had given up all hope of hearing from María Elena, she received a letter. It came exactly one year to the day that María Elena and Sebastian had disappeared together. The letter was sent to her office in San Francisco. It arrived in a plastic bag, damaged somehow in the transport. The envelope was crumpled and stained, as if it had been accidentally dropped in a puddle of solvents; the postmark was faded, obscuring its place and time of origin; the return address was blurred and illegible, and the stamp had been damaged beyond recognition. Although the envelope was damaged, the letter inside was intact, neatly typed in the angular and archaic font produced by an old typewriter. It was written in Spanish and said:

> *Querida* Rachel,
>
> I have received your messages. I have not responded since I have not been at any one place for very long, but now that has changed. You can reach me at the return address on the envelope. Forgive my delinquency. I hope you did not think harm had come to us, or worse that I no longer wished to have contact with you.
>
> I have some papers—journals of my research, drawings, and photographs—at the care of the University. I would like them turned over to you for safekeeping. The University already has a written authorization from me.
>
> In the meantime, we have sent you a picture of our son, Martín.
>
> Your devoted daughter,
>
> María Elena

Rachel Vázquez looked inside the envelope. A photograph was struck to the damaged side of the envelope and was partially destroyed. The faded image of the child was like that of one born prematurely, violently ripped from his mother's secret waters. His smallness gave him the look of a barely living creature, indistinct and primeval. Rachel moved closer to the window, hoping that the sun's natural light could refocus and magnify the dull and damaged image. The grotesque distortion of the picture and Rachel's inability to contact María Elena directly sent her into a period of melancholy and depression. She suffered from nightmares that woke her throughout the night. For the first time in her life, she experienced bouts of insomnia that unexpectedly began to spread to her husband and children as if it were a contagion.

The family was saved from its collective insomnia when, several months later, another letter from María Elena arrived. This time the postmark and return address revealed its point of origin: Tlaxcala. Rachel found the letter inside to be like the one before, typewritten in Spanish. It said:

> *Querida* Rachel,
>
> During the celebration of the Day Of the Dead, I dreamed that you were walking along a wide road, and that the planets had gotten bigger. If you should dream of that road and of those planets, Rachel, you must wake yourself immediately because it is the road that will take you to your death. Your children need you to live.
>
> *Con todo cariño*, your devoted daughter,
>
> María Elena Vázquez

These two letters from María Elena put the entire Vázquez family at ease because they assured them that she and Sebastian were alive and had, in their own manner, found fulfillment in their fugitive love.

But not Rachel. Upon learning of the address in Tlaxcala, she immediately wrote María Elena asking if they—Rachel, María Elena, and Sebastian—could meet and begin to reconcile with their family. Several days after it was mailed, the letter was returned, damaged in the same manner as María Elena's first letter: the envelope stained, the stamp torn, and the postmark blurred. As Rachel fingered the envelope, she was overcome by a strange sensation and, in a fleeting moment, saw in her mind's eye a Spanish colonial town with cobblestone streets, horse-drawn carriages and people dressed in nineteenth century attire. Rachel later told her brothers, "The letter never reached María Elena because it went back in time."

Soon thereafter, Rachel claimed that in the backgrounds of photographs and paintings in the museums of San Francisco she could see episodes of María Elena's life. Her family feared that perhaps the curse that had been placed on their Vázquez ancestors, centuries before, was insanity. But those fears were misplaced. Like Sebastian and María Elena before her, Rachel would eventually solve the mystery of her temporary madness, but only after her own journey into the peripheries of dreams and wind.

The Author

Rosa Martha Villarreal is a native Texan whose family origins in the Mexican states of Nuevo Leon and Coahuila date back to the mid-1500s. A resident of California, she is a graduate of San José State University and the author of the modern Faustian novella, *Doctor Magdalena.*

This first English language edition of *Chronicles of Air and Dreams* was printed for Archer Books in 1999 by Thomson-Shore, Inc. Typeface is Bauer Bodoni.

In 1926, under the direction of Heinrich Jost, Louis Höll cut the punches for the Bauer typefoundry's version of Bodoni. Bauer Bodoni is closest to the original Bodoni in its proportions and characteristic refinement and delicacy. Bodoni was designed by and named after the prolific Giambattista Bodoni of Parma, Italy, who designed the famous types at the end of the eighteenth century.

Interior and jacket designed, composed and set by John Taylor-Convery at JTC Imagineering.